Marty,
Next tim-
the cover at your p-
on a program that isn't
called Paintbrush. Thanks
for all your help. really
appreciate it!

NIGHT BURGER

WRITTEN AND ILLUSTRATED BY

Jason Sarna

Night Burger

Cover design: Martin J. Murphy

Editor: Rachel Lee Cherry, Last Syllable Communications

ISBN: 1495291170
ISBN-13: 978-1495291173
Library of Congress Control Number: 2014906032

Printed in the United States of America

This book is dedicated to anyone who has ever worked customer service.

"Why do people like quotes so much?"
—Tom Mitchell

- Author's Note -

I met Tom Mitchell in March 2009. He entered my body/mind and refused to release me until many years later. The views and opinions documented in this story are Tom's, and I (the lackey author) cannot be held accountable for the contents of this book as Tom made sure I wrote *his* story exactly as *he* saw it.

In 2014, I managed to exorcise Tom Mitchell from my body/mind. I have no clue as to his present whereabouts and am unsure if he will ever return.

one

HENRY'S SITTING on his E-Z-Rest recliner watching TV when I walk into our apartment. He's been sitting on that thing for eight years now. It's pretty impressive when you stop and think about it. Anything that people do for long periods of time is impressive, if you ask me.

I flick on the light and close the front door. It still smells inside. I don't think Henry's taking showers anymore. Some people refuse to take showers on purpose, as a fashion statement or something. Henry's not into fashion though. When we first moved in together, he bought, like, eighty white T-shirts and three pairs of navy jersey shorts. He's been wearing the same stuff since.

I take off my shoes and set my greasy Night Burger bag on the wooden coffee table in front of the TV.

"Hey," I say to Henry. He doesn't respond.

I walk over to the sliding glass door and crack it to get some air flowing. It's early June, so the weather outside is nice and cool, especially around midnight. I work the 3 p.m. to 11 p.m. shift at Rudy's Grocery. It takes me almost an hour to drive home. I know, it's stupid to drive that far to work at a grocery store, but I have no choice. Anyway, I hate working at Rudy's. I hate it more than anything in the world. I hate the manager, I hate the employees, and most of all, I hate the customers.

"Another great day at work!" I announce as I enter the kitchen. "I love working at Rudy's!"

I like our kitchen because it's connected to the living room, and we can talk to each other while we cook. I thought about becoming a chef once but didn't want to lose a finger. Chefs are always chopping their fingers off. Every chef wants to be the fastest chopper. It's like impressing a girl with a fast car, except they're impressing girls with a fast blade. When you're driving fast and you crash, you die. But when you're chopping fast and you crash, you lose a finger. I'd rather crash in a car and die because people with

missing fingers look weird, and if I had a missing finger, m,
life would be over. I can just imagine what people would
say: "There's that weird guy with the missing finger." Lisa
wouldn't want anything to do with me. I need to talk to her
before it's too late.

I grab a glass and fill it with water.

"We're still hiring," I say.

Once again, Henry doesn't respond. He just stares at
some soldiers shooting each other on TV.

"Have you thought any more about applying to
Rudy's?" I ask.

Still nothing.

I've known Henry since I was five years old. We met at
the bus stop. Back then, he was a chubby-cheeked kid with
short brown hair. Now his hair hangs way past his shoulders
and he has a long beard. It's been six months since he last
spoke. We didn't have a huge blowout or anything; he just
went into quiet mode for some reason.

"Lisa told me to tell you she has lots of single cashier
friends."

Nothing I tell Henry anymore is true. I've been lying to him for the past three months and telling him how Rudy's is the greatest place ever.

My latest theory about Henry's silence is that it's the result of all my negativity through the years. I've talked a lot of shit to him about customers, work, and all that stuff. That's why I'm lying and pretending to be positive. It hasn't worked so far, but I'm not giving up. The ideal situation would be if Henry got up off the E-Z-Rest and started working at Rudy's. It would be nice to have him there for backup. I'm under some fire from the three main employee groups that are at war with each other: the Old Men, the Women's Circle, and the Voyeurs.

BOOM! ZOOOOOM! "AAAAAHH!!"

A giant yellow plane just flew over the televised battlefield and blew a bunch of people away.

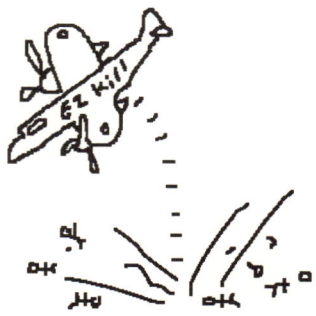

I don't think bomber planes are fair in war. It's fine if they're fighting each other, but they shouldn't be allowed to blow up people on the ground. It's just not fair. I wonder if Henry ever thought about installing a plane engine in his E-

Z-Rest. If I sat on a recliner for eight years, I'd be thinking up stuff like that all the time.

☰ ☰ ☰

I grab my Night Burger bag off the wooden coffee table, hold it up to my face, and breathe in.

"Mmm," I say. "Night Burger."

I've been eating at Night Burger a lot lately. It's actually all I've been eating. Before and after work, I stop by the drive-thru. I also go on my days off. I can't stop eating it. Henry and I used to go to Night Burger when we were kids. We both loved it and thought it was the greatest place ever.

"I got some Space Sticks here if you want any," I say as I sit on the blue couch and open the bag.

No reaction.

Space Sticks is Night Burger's name for fries. They have special names for all their food and drinks. The only thing they don't have a special name for is the burgers. They just call them "Night Burgers," which is kind of special, but not as special as Space Sticks. I worked at Night Burger back in high school, but I quit when I started fantasizing about poisoning the customers.

Before I go any further, I feel like I need to tell you who I am. People hate not knowing who people are. I know a lot about this from working at Rudy's. My name's Mitchell. Tom Mitchell. I introduce myself like that because I think it sounds cool. I'm twenty-six years old. People always tell me that I look like I'm in my mid-thirties, and that really pisses me off. And before you start going off on how my name's the stupidest name you've ever heard, I want you to know that I'm well aware. I hate my name. Tom Mitchell. It reminds me of some loser with some horrible skin disease. People should be able to pick their names once they hit twenty-five. Until then, every son should be called "son" and every daughter should be called "daughter." I never met my real parents. My fake parents are dead.

BANG! BANG!

Some unsatisfied-looking soldier just walked into a ma-and-pa store and shot both Ma and Pa right in the head. Fucking customers.

I always eat my Space Sticks first because I like getting them out of the way. It's like they're an audience, and I don't like eating in front of a bunch of people. I ate lunch in the break room at Rudy's once and I'll never do it again. Every employee staring and silently judging. One wrong bite and I could have been the laughingstock of the entire grocery store.

"Every Rudy's employee is awesome," I say. "I'll introduce you to them all."

Henry doesn't blink.

"I guarantee you eight bucks an hour."

Nope.

"There are single girls everywhere!"

Nothing.

It's like I don't know what I have to tell this kid. I'm reaching the point where I'm going to start slapping him around if he doesn't start talking soon. It's been six months. I try to deal with his silence, but there's only so much a person can take. If the situation were reversed and Henry was telling me about all these friends and girls and hefty paychecks, I would be running to Rudy's. But no, Henry's just sitting here watching this dumb war movie. If he likes war so much, he'll love Rudy's. There's nothing but war going on over there. When my shift ended today, I walked into the break room to grab my gray sweatshirt and saw two women employees holding an old man employee underneath the sink faucet. They were either trying to drown him or burn him with hot water. Whatever the case, he didn't look happy. His legs were kicking all over. I tried to grab my sweatshirt and hurry out without being noticed, but one of the women saw me and started screaming "Get out!" over and over. I had to leave my sweatshirt and drive home wearing my stupid uniform. I don't like wearing that thing in public. I need my sweatshirt back.

I finish my Space Sticks and pull out my burger. Seeing it calms me down. I need a break from everything that's going on inside my head. I peel back the gold wrapper and take a big bite.

"These urgers are stil the best," I mumble. I take another bite, chew, and swallow. "Remember the first time we went to Night Burger?"

Silence.

I throw the burger wrapper in the bag and readjust myself on the blue couch to get comfortable. The war movie looks like it's coming to an end. Everything is destroyed, and everyone is dead except for these two soldiers. Of course. Movies are so predictable. The soldiers are standing, facing one another on opposite sides of the battlefield. Their uniforms are bloody and torn, and one of them is missing a finger. I look at Henry. His eyelids are drooping. He's going to miss the best part. I refocus on the TV. The soldiers slowly walk toward one another across the fiery rubble until they are only a few feet apart.

"Look what we've done," says the fingerless soldier. His eyes scan the battlefield as the camera pans over dead bodies, destroyed buildings, abandoned guns, and dis-membered body parts. "This is wrong. The killing, the de-struction . . ." He lowers his weapon and launches into this sentimental speech about how war is pointless and how humans should cherish life and treat others with respect, but before he can deliver his full message, the other soldier pulls out a knife and stabs him right in his fingerless heart.

I wake up on the blue couch to someone screaming.

"I hold the solutions!" the voice yells. "I hold the answers! I hold the secrets to living a great life!"

It's coming from the TV. I rub my eyes and glance at Henry. His eyelids are closed and his arms hang limply over the recliner's armrests. The VCR reads: 4:42 a.m. I yawn, shift, and stare at the bright screen. I have to squint until my eyes adjust. The voice is coming from some fat guy with a bad toupee that keeps falling off his head. He's wearing a white T-shirt that says **MR. JIM** in bold, black lettering.

"My life used to be a horrible, terrible, gosh-darn mess!" he yells into a microphone on the stage of a packed auditorium. "I needed a solution to all of life's little problems. So what did I do? Sit on my couch and pout? No! I discovered the answers, and *you* can too!"

The camera cuts to the audience screaming and applauding and going mad. People shake one another. Others toss chairs onto the stage. One woman turns to this wrinkled old man next to her and kisses him right on his crusty lips. Everyone starts chanting "Mr. Jim! Mr. Jim! Mr. Jim!"

With a giant smile on his face, Mr. Jim runs around the stage, punching the air and yelling "YES!" over and over. I sit frozen, unable to look away.

"Listen up, people!" Mr. Jim announces.

The audience gets quiet.

"Six months ago, a man by the name of Rodney Johns came to me and said, 'Mr. Jim, my wife and three-month-old daughter were killed in an automobile accident, and I no longer have any reason to live.'"

The audience gasps.

"Don't worry, folks, because I have fixed Rodney Johns!"

Mr. Jim takes a bow, and his toupee falls onto the stage.

"Come on out, Rodney!" he yells, picking up his hairpiece and pressing it back into place.

Rodney takes the stage, waving like he's the president or something. Mr. Jim passes him the microphone. "Mr. Jim fixed me," he says. "After my wife and daughter were killed, I didn't want to live. But now, thanks to Mr. Jim, I am remarried and my new wife and I are trying to create a new daughter."

The audience rises to its feet, applauding wildly as Mr. Jim takes Rodney's hand and lifts it triumphantly toward the sky. An 800 number flashes on the screen. For just four easy payments of $19.99, plus $4.95 shipping and handling, I can get Mr. Jim's Life Improvement Kit.

I jump off the couch and run into my bedroom to grab a pen. I hurry back into the living room, rip off a piece of my Night Burger bag, and write down the number. I look at Henry. He's still passed out. *This will definitely be a good investment.* I thought about turning the TV off, but Henry likes to sleep with it on. I flick off the living room lights, close the sliding glass door, and go to bed.

two

"INTRODUCE YOURSELF, Tom."

"Hello." I paused. My mom nudged me on the back. "I'm Tom."

"Henry."

We shook hands. Our moms started talking. Henry and I stood staring at one another. He was bigger than me, taller and wider. His short brown hair was combed to the side and he was dressed in blue jeans and a gray sweatshirt. Strapped to his back was this bright red backpack.

"It's called a rabbit's foot," Henry's mom said as she handed my mom this small furry trinket.

"It's so soft."

I looked back at Henry. He picked up a handful of rocks and started tossing them down the street.

"Do you live on Dixie Court?" he asked.

I nodded.

Henry turned and whipped a rock down the road.

"I live over there," he said. "The brown house with the curved driveway."

He lived right off Circle Trail. The school bus stop met where the two streets intersected.

"You should come over sometime."

"Sure."

≧ ≧ ≧

The front door opened and Henry was standing there.

"Hello," he said.

"Hello," I said.

My mom hugged me good-bye. "Be good," she told me. "I'll pick you up around five."

I walked inside and took off my shoes. The house was dark and quiet.

"Where are your parents?" I asked.

"My dad's at work and my mom's upstairs."

We walked past the kitchen and through the living room, then down a long hallway that led to his bedroom. It was huge. Twice the size of mine. Taped to the walls were hundreds of these strange bed-chair pictures.

"What are all these pictures of?" I asked.

"They're called E-Z-Rest recliners," Henry said as he closed his bedroom door. "I'm asking for one this Christmas."

The recliners came in every color: blue, gray, yellow, red, brown, everything. The cushions looked super puffy, and on the lower right side of the frame was a small wooden handle. In some of the pictures, people were sitting on the recliners. They all had gigantic smiles on their faces.

"You want a tour?" Henry asked

"Sure."

We walked around his bedroom and closely examined each recliner picture. He explained the different styles, functions, and fabric options and answered all my questions in great detail.

"This one's my favorite," he said, pointing to the puffy gray one that was taped above his bed. "I acquired it from my mom's *Suburban Living* magazine."

"Why's it your favorite?" I asked.

"I'm not sure," he replied. "But I feel a connection with it."

At the end of the tour, Henry made me promise to always remember one thing: "If it's not an E-Z-Rest, it's not a real recliner."

We spent the rest of the afternoon lying on the bedroom carpet imagining a world filled with recliners. We closed our eyes and drifted off to a place where every chair transformed into a comfy bed with the pull of a wooden lever. We erased all we knew about the world we lived in. We got rid of trees, schools, houses, plants, bugs, animals, and even people, and we replaced everything with E-Z-Rest recliners. It was the perfect world. We were free to sit wherever we wanted. Anything was possible. There were no parents, no teachers, no one to tell us what to do, when to go to bed or how many times a day we're supposed to brush our teeth. We were kings—the most comfortable kings in all the land.

"All hail King Tom!" I yelled.

"All hail King Henry!" Henry yelled.

Every now and again Henry and I would open our eyes, look at each other, and smile. This E-Z-Rest World was special. It was something we had both created—a secret place that no one else knew existed.

Kindergarten wasn't my favorite. I liked the scissor cutting and gluing parts, but that was about it. Henry and I were in separate classes. I barely talked to any of the other kids. We had nothing in common. They didn't talk about any of the stuff Henry and I talked about, and they knew nothing about E-Z-Rests.

"How can a chair also be a bed?" they would ask me.

"Forget it."

The best part of kindergarten was when the school day ended and Henry and I were able to hang out together. Our two main activities were talking about E-Z-Rests and watching cable TV. *Abduction* was our favorite show. It was about random kids getting abducted by strangers and being taken to these cool new worlds. One time, we stood at the edge of Henry's driveway waiting for someone to pick us up and transport us to our E-Z-Rest World. A bunch of cars drove past, but none of them ever stopped.

"Don't talk too much."

"Don't run inside."

"Don't annoy his parents."

Whenever my mom walked me to Henry's house, she went over this list of rules.

"Don't chew with your mouth open."

"Don't yell."

"Don't ask too many questions."

I spent a lot of time at Henry's, so it was important that I act right. I think my mom was afraid that I would slip up and ruin the family name, which was weird because I didn't even have the same last name as her and my dad. Their last name was Lexington. Mine was Mitchell. They told me early on that I was adopted so, according to my mom, "things don't get weird in the later years."

Our first sleepover was on Halloween night. Henry's mom took us trick-or-treating around the neighborhood. We both dressed up as E-Z-Rest owners. It was an easy costume. All we did was dress in normal clothes and walk around with gigantic smiles on our faces. We stayed up late eating candy and fell asleep in the living room watching scary movies.

The next morning, I awoke to loud yelling. It was coming from upstairs. I lifted my head off my pillow and looked at Henry. He was still asleep on the couch. The TV was on, and there were candy wrappers all over. The yelling continued.

"Henry," I whispered. "Wake up."

His eyelids opened.

"Do you hear that?" I asked.

He listened for a second. *More loud yelling.* "Let's go."

We grabbed our candy bags, blankets, and pillows and walked down the long hallway into Henry's bedroom. He closed the door.

"What's going on?" I asked.

"It's my parents."

"Why are they yelling?"

Henry set his candy bag on the carpet and crawled into his bed. "They're always yelling."

"About what?" I asked as I set my blanket and pillow on the floor.

"Fur coats," he replied.

I sat and pulled a tiny chocolate bar from my candy bag. "What's a fur coat?"

"I guess it's a coat made out of fur."

"What kind of fur?"

"Animal fur," said Henry.

"They're shaving animals?"

"I'm not sure how it works. I just know my mom really wants one but my dad doesn't want to buy it."

A month or so before Christmas, Henry started taking down some of his E-Z-Rest pictures.

"What are you doing?" I asked.

"I'm leaving these around the house so my parents find them."

"Why?"

"So they know what I want for Christmas."

"Can I have one?"

Henry hesitated but eventually handed one over.

I took the recliner picture home and left it on the kitchen table. My mom found it while preparing dinner and asked me if it was mine.

"Yes," I said.

"Put it in your room or it's going in the trash."

Neither of us got an E-Z-Rest that Christmas. I wasn't too upset about it, but Henry was a different story. He was devastated. I wasn't exactly sure why, because his parents bought him a brand-new TV and VCR for his bedroom. All I got for Christmas were some new tops and a pair of jeans. Henry also got a red race car bed. I thought it was great, but Henry hated it. He told me the only reason his parents got him the *stupid* car bed was because his dad owned a used car dealership and got *stupid* car beds for cheap.

"I wish he owned a used E-Z-Rest dealership," Henry said, wiping tears from his face.

"Do your parents have a race car bed too?" I asked.

"No, they just have a regular one."

It didn't make sense to me why Henry's parents didn't have a race car bed, especially if his dad got them for cheap. My parents bought everything for cheap. If it wasn't on sale, it wasn't worth their time. That's what my mom always said. She made me clip coupons with her every Sunday. I didn't mind because I was great with scissors. My mom did all the shopping and housework and talked on the phone to some woman named Ruth all the time. My dad worked at this factory called Teltrox that manufactured women's pantyhose. I'm sure he got pantyhose for cheap, but I had no use for pantyhose because I wasn't a girl.

"Are you okay?" I asked Henry.

He was standing in front of his new TV and flipping channels. "No." His face was all red from crying.

"Just ask for the E-Z-Rest next year," I said.

Henry shook his head. "You don't understand."

three

THE NEXT MORNING, Henry and his E-Z-Rest were gone. His recliner left a dark circular imprint in the carpet that reminded me of one of those UFO crop circles. I found one of those back when I was a kid. It was out in this tall grassy field behind my fake parents' house. I never told anyone about it because I knew that humans weren't friendly with aliens. I visited the crop circle a bunch to see if the spaceship would return. It never did. The grass eventually grew back and the circle disappeared.

"Henry!" I call out.

The apartment's silent. Even the TV's turned off. The TV's never turned off. It's against Henry's beliefs. He once told me that turning off a TV is like murder.

"HENRY!"

I search for a good-bye note. People typically leave good-bye notes whenever they leave town. I'm not sure if Henry left town or not, but something happened. Maybe he actually installed a plane engine in his E-Z-Rest and took off to some faraway land. I wouldn't doubt it. Dire's a horrible town to live in. I'm surprised he didn't take the TV with him. He probably didn't have any room for it. You can't pack much when you're flying around on a recliner.

I give up on my search, sit on the blue couch, and stare at the blank TV screen. I think about calling Henry's mom, but I haven't talked to her in forever. Henry and his mom aren't exactly close. They haven't spoken to or seen one another in years. She sends him a check every month for $2,000. Folded around the checks are pictures of new E-Z-Rest recliners with notes that read like this:

- *You'd sit great on this*
- *Here's a little something extra for your comfort*
- *This seat's on me*

The notes always annoy me. The sayings are stupid. My recliner note would say something like *You look beat, have a seat.* That's not even that great, but at least it rhymes.

The front door opens and Henry walks inside carrying a bunch of plastic bags from Vick's Produce.

"Hello, Tom," he says as he kicks the front door closed.

I can't believe it's him. His face is shaved. His hair's cut short. He looks like a completely different person. I also can't believe his first words to me were "Hello, Tom." We never say hello to one another. We're not into that crap.

Henry sets his grocery bags on the kitchen counter and displays his new self to me. "So . . . how do I look?"

He's wearing a blue button-down shirt tucked into a pair of khaki pants and shiny black dress shoes. He doesn't look anything like my friend. The Henry I know wears navy jersey shorts and white T-shirts and has a big beard and long hair. This Henry is all dressed up and adult-looking.

"Well?"

"You look good," I lie.

"Thanks."

Henry smiles and enters the kitchen. *I need to play this right.* I don't want to say the wrong thing or ask him too many questions. I know about the human psyche and it's very complex. Whenever people come out of life-changing situations, you have to be extremely careful. Henry's like a wild bird right now. If I talk too loudly or make any sudden moves, he might fly away again.

I remain on the blue couch and observe the bird-human from a distance.

"I bought more milk," Henry says as he opens the refrigerator. "That other stuff was expired."

"Cool."

I don't even drink milk. I don't even buy groceries. I haven't been grocery shopping for months. You would think that, since I work at a grocery store, I'm shopping all the time. Not true. Working at a grocery store has ruined grocery shopping for me. I can't stand it—the carts, the customers, the *beep beep beep* of the cash registers. It's like that for everyone. Like, if I sold plastics, I would never use plastics. No way. I would hate plastics. That's just how it works.

Henry finishes putting away his groceries and sits at the small plastic kitchen table we never use. He's holding a tiny orange cup-looking thing.

"What is that?" I ask.

"Yogurt."

I've known Henry for twenty-one years and I've never seen him eat anything healthy. He's supposed to be eating chips and candy and other junk food. I don't want my best friend eating yogurt.

"You don't eat yogurt," I say.

"I'm trying to eat more healthy," he replies. "I also bought some apples, oranges, frozen vegetables, and low-fat micro meals."

I want to jump off the couch and strangle him, but I can't. He's too intimidating with his new clothes and adult haircut and healthy food choices. I don't even know if this is the *real* Henry. I've read a lot of science fiction, and body switching is something I know a little about.

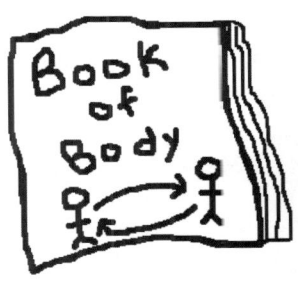

"Only one hundred and thirty calories. Calcium. B12. Vitamins."

"What are you talking about?" I ask.

"Those are the ingredients," says Henry.

He doesn't even know what any of that stuff means. *He's lying to himself!* I push myself off the blue couch and turn on the TV. Nothing but black-and-white fuzz.

"Oh, yeah!" Henry yells. "I canceled the cable earlier this morning."

"What?!" I yell back.

I don't even bother turning around to look at him. I just stare into the fuzzy screen, listening to the static.

"I'm done with TV," he states.

"I'm not."

"Well, I was paying for it."

I knew that whole paying-the-bills business was too good to be true. He did it just to own me and have all the power.

"So what if I want to watch TV?" I ask.

"Pick up a set of bunny ears," he tells me. "That will get you the local stations."

That's a direct hit. Henry *knows* that all the local stations suck.

"Maybe I'll do that!" I shout.

I want to remind him of his belief that turning off a TV is like murder. He hadn't just turned off the TV, though. He canceled the cable. He's worse than a murderer. He's a fucking serial killer.

☰ ☰ ☰

I turn off the TV.

"I'm going to work," I say.

"I'll go with you," Henry replies.

I turn around.

"Why?"

"I'm going to apply."

I pause.

"I have to use the bathroom."

"Oh, that reminds me—" Henry stands and walks into the kitchen. "I have to take my vitamins."

I flick on the bathroom lights and close the door. I was so thrown off by the new Henry that I wasn't even thinking about Rudy's or the three main employee groups or any of that stuff. My mind works like that sometimes. It forgets major details when I'm focused on something else. Whatever. My positivity plan worked. Henry's talking again and wants to apply to Rudy's. He'll get the job. I wish he were acting normal. I'll have to adapt to his new look and healthy outlook. He does need to lose weight. He's pushing 300 pounds. I'm sure he'll be back to his old self any day now. He'll get the cable hooked back up and buy one of those fancy new E-Z-Rests. Maybe his mom finally sent him a picture he liked.

Before leaving, I tell Henry not to mention my name on the application or during the interview process.

"Why not?" he asks. "You told me that all I have to do is mention your name and I'll get the job."

I did tell him that. I told him lots of things.

"Yeah," I say. "But there have been some problems lately."

"What kind of problems?"

"You know . . ." *I've been stealing toilet paper out of the employee bathroom and think my manager, Pete, is on to me.* "Sometimes companies don't like to hire friends because when friends work together, they end up goofing off."

"You're goofing off?"

"No. Listen. Just don't mention my name."

Henry nods. "I don't want to be associated with a troublemaker."

four

HENRY SAT on his red race car bed and flipped through TV channels while I sat on the carpet. He still had a bunch of E-Z-Rest pictures taped to the walls. He told me he wasn't going to let his parents ruin his dreams.

"Stop!"

Henry stopped flipping channels. "What?"

"Click back a few," I said.

He changed the station.

"No."

He changed the station again—"No."—and again—"No."—and again. "There!"

"What is this?" Henry asked.

"I'm not sure," I said. "It looks like some music show."

On the TV were several well-dressed people sitting in chairs playing these weird, twisted instruments. The music wasn't like anything I'd ever heard. Facing the people playing the instruments was some crazy-looking guy with poofy gray hair waving around a small stick and moving his body with the music.

"That guy looks funny," I said.

"I like how he makes those faces," Henry replied.

When the show ended, Henry jumped off his bed and went straight for his closet. He pulled out a shoebox full of markers and we each grabbed one. I lifted a blue marker high into the air and—

"Stop!"

I stood frozen as Henry walked over to his cassette player. "We need some music."

He didn't have anything like the stuff we heard on TV, so we conducted to a disco tape that belonged to his mom.

Henry and I loved conducting and began doing it regularly. On weekdays, we'd practice by ourselves. I would listen to the radio and record the songs I enjoyed. I would then practice conducting those songs alone in my bedroom. Henry did the same. On weekends, I would sleep over at Henry's and we would perform private conducting concerts for one another in his room. It was fun and made us feel good inside. We would often talk about how awesome it would be to become a professional music conductor—if we were *both* conductors. We created lives and identities for ourselves. We knew where we were going to live, who our wives were, how many kids we would have, and when we would retire. Our many talks and big dreams urged us to learn more about conducting, as we desperately wanted to become part of the conducting world.

We eventually decided that the best way to learn about conducting was to go down to the local video store to see if they had any movies on it. Tony's Video was the only video store in Glenshire. It was owned and operated by some big bearded guy named Howie. According to Henry, who heard it from his dad, Tony and Howie were brothers. Tony opened the store in the mid-seventies and ran it until he was tragically killed while shooting a live-action car stunt for some movie he and Howie were filming. After his brother's death, Howie stepped in and took over as owner.

The inside of the video store was decorated with all sorts of movie posters and smelled like pizza. Howie sat behind the front counter watching some action flick on a tiny TV set. I could hear gunshots and explosions going off as people screamed for their lives.

"Welcome, little guys," said Howie. "Let me know if you need any help."

Henry and I smiled and waved, as we knew exactly what we were looking for and figured we could find it ourselves.

After about ten minutes of searching and coming up empty-handed, we realized that we needed Howie's help.

"Excuse me," Henry said.

Howie paused the movie he was watching. "What's up, little guys?"

We explained how we were interested in getting into music conducting and wondered if there were any movies on it.

"You *both* want to conduct?" he asked.

Henry and I nodded.

"That's cool. My brother and I used to make movies." Howie stepped out from behind the counter. "Come on."

We followed Howie through the maze of videos until he stopped at one of the aisles.

"Okay, it's right . . . around . . . *here*."

He grabbed an empty movie box from the top shelf and handed it to Henry. "It's called *Conduct This*. I've heard good things."

Henry and I left the video store pumped. We were one step closer to our dreams. Soon we would be on the inside and know everything about conducting. We ran the rest of the way to Henry's house and popped the movie into his VCR as soon as we got inside. While Henry fast-forwarded through the coming attractions, we discussed what would be on the tape.

"I hope they teach us how to professionally conduct," Henry said.

"I want to see what kind of cars conductors drive!" I yelled.

The movie was narrated by this sleepy-eyed guy named Wes Pennington. He was a retired conductor who had been in the business more than thirty years. He told us that he was happy to tell the true story of the conductor and explained that the movie would be presented in two parts.

Part 1: Conducting 101

In this part, we learned about hand movements and how they were vital to the musical performance. The conductor typically uses either a wooden or plastic conducting baton and waves it in specific rhythmic movements to keep everyone on track with the music. He traces the air with his baton to cue musicians and change tempo and volume throughout the piece. He also incorporates his body and facial features into the performance by moving around and letting his gestures speak to the orchestra. When his body moves slowly and his face saddens, the entire pace of the musical piece should decrease and the musicians should play a little quieter. If his body moves faster and anger strikes his face, the orchestra should play louder and more powerfully.

This part also explained conductor school and the importance of good hearing. Wes highly advised against listening to music with headphones, shooting guns, and working with small children. Average conductor salary, how to get hired, best practices, work schedules, and other technicalities were also discussed.

Part 2: The Personal Lives of Conductors

According to Wes, many music conductors partied harder than the wildest rock bands. He compared their wild lifestyles to groups like Stick Figure, Black Road, and X. There were interviews with various band members talking about how conductors made rock stars look like saints. The lead singer of X, Rick Magnet, claimed that a conductor named Gus Tellock got him addicted to heroin. When asked where Gus was now, Rick said, "Dead. Dude died from a heroin overdose."

Dr. Franklin Penning, the movie psychologist, provided an explanation for the conductors' extreme behavior. He described how the constant stress of conducting led to their crazy lifestyles. It turned out that many professional conductors took their job way too seriously and were known to be obsessive about their work. Every detail had to be perfect and exactly how they envisioned it in their minds. If the smallest thing was off, it would send them into a complete frenzy, which oftentimes led to the conductor violently pulling at his hair until it permanently shot straight up toward the sky.

Most music conductors fell prey to the profession. The pressure to be great and perform brilliantly caused weakness and insecurity to flood their musical veins and blacken their sensitive hearts. Many conductors abandoned their friends and families to spend their days alone curled up on the cold floors of their offices with drool and spit running down their rabid mouths. Many conductors became completely isolated from the world. Many went insane, many overdosed on drugs, and many simply killed themselves.

When the video ended, Henry and I sat on his bedroom floor in silence watching the credits roll by until the screen went black and the VCR started rewinding. I could see my reflection and Henry's in the empty TV screen. Even though we didn't say anything, it was like we made a silent agreement that we would never let that happen. We would never get that crazy about a job or stop being friends or kill ourselves. We didn't want anything to do with that. We just wanted to have fun.

As soon as the VCR stopped rewinding, Henry got up and put the tape in its clear plastic case. We never conducted again.

five

THE LAST TIME I saw Henry, he was walking into Rudy's to apply for the job. That was over ten hours ago. I thought he'd be home when I returned from work, but no, the apartment's empty. I have no idea where he is. He probably got lost on his drive home or something. When people sit for long periods of time, they forget how to do things. I would go look for him, but I've already taken my shoes off. Some people never take their shoes off. They wear them while walking, sitting, showering. The other day I saw an advertisement for a pair of shoes that help people sleep better. It's the same idea as shoes that make people better at sports. I thought about buying a pair of these sleep shoes, but they cost, like, $200. I don't have that kind of money. If I did, I'd reactivate the cable so I could do something besides think about shoes.

Henry strolls in around 1 a.m. I'm sitting on the blue couch waiting.

"Where were you?" I ask.

"I got the job!"

"What?"

"I got the job!" he repeats. "I start tomorrow."

He closes the front door and heads into the kitchen.

"So where were you this whole time?"

He opens the refrigerator.

"Celebrating," he says.

"By yourself?"

"I was hanging out with this guy, Mike, who works mornings."

"How do you know him?"

"He was in the office during the interview."

Henry sits at the small plastic kitchen table we never use. He's eating that yogurt crap again.

"Does this Mike know me?" I ask.

"How would I know?"

"Well . . . did you mention my name?"

"You said not to tell anyone that I knew you."

"Nice!" I yell. "Real nice!"

"What's that about?" Henry asks as he peels off the yogurt lid.

"What's what about?"

"That tone."

"I'm not giving you a tone."

I remain on the couch and watch Henry shovel spoonful after spoonful of yogurt into his mouth. Astronauts eat everything in yogurt form. If Henry were an astronaut, I wouldn't mind him eating yogurt, but the reality is Henry's not a fucking astronaut.

"So what's this Mike like?" I ask.

"He's cool, likes to joke a lot."

"Is he funny?"

"Yeah," Henry says.

"I don't talk to any morning shift people," I say. "They're all weirdoes."

"Why's that?"

"Trust me. They're bad news."

"Mike seems like a cool guy."

Henry angles the yogurt container and scrapes inside with his spoon.

"Stay away from him," I demand.

Henry shoots me a weird look. "We're supposed to hang out this Friday after work."

"CANCEL IT!"

"What's your problem?"

"Nothing," I say.

Henry stands and enters the kitchen.

"Are you even happy that I got the job?"

"Of course."

"You're not acting like it," he says. "All you're talking about is how I shouldn't hang out with Mike."

"I didn't know you'd be making friends already."

"That's what happens when you talk to people." Henry grabs a glass and fills it with water.

"You don't *have* to talk to people."

"Look, Tom, I'm trying to start a new life here. If people talk to me, I'm going to talk to them. I'm not going to be that weird guy who stands around and doesn't say anything, you know?"

"Yeah," I say. "You don't want to be that guy."

Henry finishes his water and sets the glass in the sink.

"So when will I meet your friends?" he asks.

"Huh?"

"All those friends at Rudy's you're always talking about."

"Oh, yeah," I say as I push myself off the blue couch and walk toward my bedroom. "Tomorrow, I guess."

I can't sleep. My mind won't shut off. This Mike guy will destroy me. Henry thinks I'm super popular at Rudy's. I'm not. I'm nothing. I've worked there something like six years and haven't made a single friend. I'm horrible at making friends. Henry's great at it. He'll probably average one new friend a day. That's five new friends per work week and about twenty new friends a month. In six years, he's going to have, like, a million friends. I'll be forgotten. I should start playing the lottery. If I were rich, making friends would be easy. My face would be in all the newspapers and on every TV station. Complete strangers would be calling me on the street: "Hey, look, everyone! It's lottery winner Tom Mitchell!" I'd probably change my name to something like Vince Kemper. I always thought Vince was a strong name, and Kemper just sounds cool. People would call me Kemp for short.

"Yo, Kemp!"

"What's up?"

"Are you wearing those sleep shoes?"

"You know it!"

I fell asleep shortly after that.

six

ON HENRY'S EIGHTH BIRTHDAY, his parents bought him a chrome BMX bike with off-road tires and blue handgrips.

"Wow!" I said when he showed up with it at my house. "This is great!"

Henry shrugged. "I guess."

I stood at the end of my driveway while Henry rode in circles around the cul-de-sac. He must have been practicing before he came over, because he knew exactly what he was doing.

"You want to try it?" Henry asked a few minutes later.

"Sure."

I grabbed the blue handgrips and threw my leg over the shiny frame.

"Just be careful," he warned. "It's not that easy at first."

I put my feet on the pedals and pushed forward. The handlebars started shaking and I crashed to the ground.

Henry ran to my side. "Are you okay?"

"That was awesome."

At dinner that night, I told my parents about Henry's new bike and how I wanted a bike for my eighth birthday.

"I don't know, Tom," said my mom. "Bikes are expensive."

"Please," I begged. "You won't have to buy me anything ever again."

My mom looked at my dad. "What do you think about this bike business?" she asked.

He set down his fork and looked up at me. "We'll see."

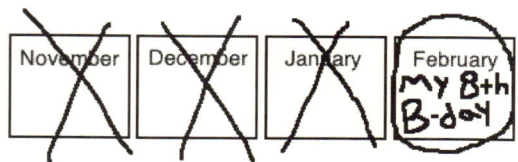

My parents actually came through and surprised me with this tall gold bike with skinny tires and white curled-down handlebars.

"You like it?" asked my mom.

"It looks a lot different from Henry's BMX."

"It's called a ten-speed," said my dad.

I walked up to the giant frame. The seat was up to my shoulders.

"I'm going in," declared my mom. "It's freezing out here."

My dad and I grabbed our winter coats from inside and returned to the garage. He told me he purchased the bike from his work buddy Ron. "We wanted to get you a BMX like Henry's," he said, "but they were much too expensive."

He assured me the ten-speed was in tip-top shape and explained how everything worked: switching gears, adjusting the seat, putting air in the tires, braking, reattaching the chain, and how leaving it out in the rain can lead to rust.

"Any questions?" he asked.

I stood staring at the giant bike. "How am I supposed to get on it?"

It took a solid month of practice and stretching before I could actually ride the ten-speed. Henry couldn't stop laughing the first time we rode together.

"What's so funny?" I asked.

"Your feet barely reach the pedals."

Come spring, an entire world opened up that neither of us knew existed. We pedaled fast through the streets of Glenshire and saw shops and people and subdivisions we had never seen before. Life was perfect. Henry and I both had bikes, and we were cruising through life without thinking about life. We lived in a world where nothing—not our parents, school, homework, E-Z-Rests, music conductors, or anything else—could hold us back. Every day, a new adventure. Every day, a new discovery. Every day, till the end of time—unless one of us got a flat tire, which happened every so often.

seven

I PULL MY CAR into the Night Burger drive-thru and roll down the window.

"Greetings, earthlings! Welcome to Night Burger!"

"Hi, I'll have the Burger Classic meal with a Saturn Fizz," I say into the moon speaker box.

"Anything else?"

"No, thanks."

"Your total is four eighty-two. Please pull your spacecraft up to the eye of the universe."

I lift my foot off the brake pedal and drive around the small curve. As I wait for my food, I think about Henry and how he should be here with me. When I woke up this morning, he was already gone. A handwritten note was left on the E-Z-Rest carpet circle:

Tom,

Since we've been pretending not to know each other, I'll come up to you today at work and introduce myself.

Henry

It's not fair. I should be the one doing the introductions. Rookies don't introduce themselves to veterans. That's not how life works. Once again, he wants all the control. It's just like with the cable TV.

The round drive-thru window a.k.a. eye of the universe opens. "Four eighty-two," says the Night Burger employee.

I hand over the money in exchange for the food. "Thanks."

I reach into my Night Burger bag and grab some Space Sticks. I don't usually eat while driving, but as soon as I get to Rudy's, I need to find Henry before he makes any more friends. It's important that I isolate him and get him on my side before one of the groups moves in and ruins everything.

Forty percent of all Rudy's afternoon shift employees are High School and College Kids. Since I work afternoons, I have no choice but to deal with it. I'm not even that much older than them, but they treat me like I'm their dad. If I walk down an aisle and there's a bunch of them standing around, they take off running. The only good thing about their group is Lisa. I don't understand why she hangs out with them. She looks around the same age as me, but I've never talked to her, so I'm not sure. Aside from that, their group is pretty much useless. They don't have a leader or anything and are the only group that's *not* involved in the war. I doubt they're even aware that there's a war going on. They live in their own world and are way too self-involved to know anything.

Another twenty percent of all Rudy's afternoon shift employees belong to a group called the Old Men. They control the back room and keep track of the entire store inventory. When I was first hired, Stan, the back room door guard, gave me a Back Room Guidebook written by their leader, Walter. I was given one week to memorize it. After the week passed, Stan brought me into the back room (blindfolded, of course) and verbally quizzed me on everything from how to get my grocery stock to taking out the trash. I barely passed. I messed up big time on the Knocking Verification System.

Most of the Old Men keep to themselves. A lot of them don't even enter through the main entrance. They park their cars around back and enter through there. Identity theft is a big concern for them. They think that showing their faces will lead to problems. I don't even know what most of the Old Men look like. I've never seen their leader before, either. The giant, powerful, all-knowing Walter might not even exist. The only old man I see on a regular basis is Stan. Like I said, he's in charge of guarding the back room doors and making sure no unauthorized personnel enter. I'm surprised they put him in charge of such an important task. He's a small, frail, gray-haired guy with a hunched back. Supposedly, though, he fought in the Big War and knows how to kill a man in more than a thousand ways.

Over the past few months, when the war started picking up, the Old Men abandoned their fifty-plus age requirement and started recruiting younger men. This angered the Women's Circle and the Voyeurs. Both sides claimed that lowering the age requirement was against wartime rules. I didn't even know there were *rules* during war. Anyway, ever since the change, Stan's been bugging me to join. It'd be nice to work in the back room, away from all the customers, but I don't think I can stand hanging out with those guys. I've overheard some of their conversations. All they talk about is the weather.

"Gonna be cold tomorrow."

"How cold?"

"Thirty-five degrees."

"That's ten degrees colder than today."

"And fifteen degrees colder than yesterday."

"We talking any sun?"

"Partly cloudy."

"Any chance of snow?"

"We're clear for now."

"Thank God for that."

"Don't need that."

"Sick of that."

"Tired of that."

If I had to listen to that nonsense on a daily basis, I'd kill myself. Some people would probably kill the weather-talking Old Men, but since I follow a No-Bother Policy[*], I can't do that. I told Stan that I didn't really want to join the

---

[*] The No-Bother Policy states that nobody should bother anyone. For instance, I don't bother people; therefore, people shouldn't bother me. I adopted this policy after working at Night Burger and have been following it ever since. It's a great policy, but no one else seems to follow it.

group because I didn't think it was for me. He wasn't too thrilled with my response and warned that Walter had looked deep into my mind and found out some pretty bad stuff.

"Your mind's the worst we've ever come across, Mr. Mitchell," Stan informed me.

I thought he was lying about all that mind-reading crap, but when he told me about the time I'd imagined bashing some customer over the head with a can of chili, I knew he was telling the truth. What impressed me most was that he knew the actual brand name of chili that I imagined using: Bergen's Chili. Stan warns that if I don't join the Old Men soon, they'll reveal my violent customer thoughts to the world.

The second largest and most powerful group at Rudy's is the Women's Circle. They make up about thirty percent of all afternoon shift employees and control all sorts of areas on the grocery floor, including eight of the ten cash registers. This is a big deal because it allows the women to raise extra money for their group by overcharging customers. They use the illegal earnings for bribes, clothes, and weapons. Controlling the registers also gives the Women's Circle easy access to the store intercom system. Each register lane is equipped with an intercom phone, which the women use to call out code words during surprise attacks and other missions.

Their leader is a tall, black-haired woman named Raven. She has dark eyes and long fingernails that can rip your face off. She's a ruthless leader who has no problem taking out one of her own. Over the years, many internal fights have ensued over power and leadership, but Raven always finds a way to exterminate the troublemakers and reconnect the group. She has held onto her title as leader by using her grocery floor smarts to stay one step ahead. With her strength, perseverance, and intelligence, she has built one of the largest and strongest groups in Rudy's history. The women who follow her are loyal and willing to do whatever it takes to win the war.

Out of all the groups, I like the Women's Circle the best. They're not bad as long as you know how to talk around them. Whenever they're nearby, I say as little as possible so as not to incriminate myself. They love to gossip. If you need to know anything about anyone, they're the ones to go to. As far as I know, all they've got on me is that I'm single, have no friends, and live in Dire. They also know my real age. I like that.

Members belonging to this group are most famous for their exceptional hearing and ability to pick up on conversations up to three aisles away. They can also hear through walls, which scares the crap out of the Old Men. Any and all information they gather is transcribed and filed away in a secret storage facility. Whenever threatened, they refer to the files and spread confidential information through the grocery store like a virus, twisting details however they please. Their rumors have gotten employees fired, banned from various cities, and even killed.

Ever since the Old Men changed their age requirement, Raven has been bugging me to join the Women's Circle. I'm not sure why. They have a strict no-male policy. I can tell some of the women are angry about the invitation. When I bought a can of Sip-Zop Pop the other day, the woman running the cash register charged me seven dollars. I didn't want to argue, so I just paid it. The money will probably be spent on guns or a new pair of shoes.

I would definitely join the Women's Circle if the Old Men and the Voyeurs weren't around. Raven claims she can protect me from both groups, but I'm not sure if I can trust her. I don't have anything against people with bird names, but there is something strange about it. She keeps on me every day, telling me I need to make up my mind about joining because the women are "getting hungry." I'm not quite sure what she means, exactly, but I'm assuming they're planning on eating me alive.

The last and smallest group is the Voyeurs. They make up only ten percent of all afternoon shift employees. They are the failed artists at Rudy's. Anyone is welcome to join the group as long as he or she enjoys spying on customers and has a *thing*. This *thing* can be anything. For instance, one voyeur, James, likes singing "Happy Birthday" to himself while watching customers shop. Another voyeur, Wendy, only spies on customers in the pet aisle while wearing a dog collar around her neck.

The leader of this group calls himself Gary. He reminds me of a matador in that he's skinny, short, and has jet-black hair that he slicks back with Silk Shine hair dressing. He sports a dark pencil-thin mustache and wears tight red pants that the women love.

All the women say

"Oh those pants!"

Directly under Gary's command are Steve a.k.a. Peek and Cory the Cork. Steve is a thirty-eight-year-old divorcé who lives a mile down the road in a run-down condo complex. He has blond hair and a brown mustache, which really baffles some of the women.

"I think he dyes it."

"You think so?"

"I think so."

"I don't think so."

Anyway, Steve's called Peek because he has excellent vision and can see through the tiniest of cracks, holes, etc., making him extremely dangerous to customers and opposing groups. Word on the grocery floor is that Peek has gained some insider information about what exactly goes on in the back room where the Old Men work.

The Women's Circle assigned Gary's other main guy the name Cory the Cork because he constantly has a butt plug up his ass. That must be his *thing*. I guess one of the women walked into the break room while he was eating and his chair started vibrating. When she found out that he didn't own a cell phone, she figured it was a butt plug.

"He must have it on some sort of timer," claimed the woman.

I'd never heard of a butt plug that was on a timer, but they have timers on watches, so why not timers on butt plugs? I'm not exactly sure how Cory's useful to Gary's whole operation, but he must bring something to the table.

The main difference between Gary and the other voyeurs is that he interacts with the customers he watches. Supposedly, he can make himself cum without touching his penis. All he has to do is physically touch some unsuspecting customer and he cums his pants. At first, I didn't believe it, but then I saw him in action. I was stocking some Gender Farm Spaghetti when I heard a woman scream a few aisles over. I ran to see what was going on and saw some customer holding Gary in her arms. His body was shaking like he was having a seizure. She had no idea he was cumming his pants.

The Voyeurs see everything that goes on at Rudy's. They are known for their amazing eyesight and ability to appear invisible. They are stealth organizers of attacks and can take out large groups without being noticed. War typically isn't their *thing*, but the idea of being able to spy on customers anywhere in the store really gets their juices flowing. Out of all three groups, I fear the Voyeurs most. They know about me using the Magic O's cereal box as a Face Blocker[*] to spy on Lisa, and they've threatened to expose me if I don't join them. If word got out that I was spying on an employee, everyone would turn against me. Employee voyeurism is strictly forbidden at Rudy's and punished severely. A long time ago, when the three main groups emerged, the founding leader of the Voyeurs (who was also named Gary) made a pact with the Old Men and the Women's Circle to only watch customers. Since all employees hate customers, they agreed. The current Gary reminds me of this pact each day.

The afternoon shift manager at Rudy's is named Pete. He's his own group. No employee wants to or will ever be a member of his bullshit club. He's a round, sweaty, balding man in his late thirties who wears prescription gold-rimmed

---

[*] A Face Blocker is any store item used to block one's face.

aviator eyeglasses and carries around a black-and-white polka-dot handkerchief. He's always snooping around trying to find out what's going on, but no one tells him the truth about anything. He once told me, back when I first started, that I'd make "a good little Pete one day." I hope not. Pete's a by-the-book type of guy and strictly adheres to all of Rudy's ridiculous policies. He believes customers are number one and should be treated with respect at all times. The man has no brain. He lives in his own pathetic reality and pretends that he's making some big difference in the world by working as a stupid shift manager. He loves eating Zolo's Chips, which come in an orange and blue bag and are doused with Captain Zolo's fire sauce. Every time he eats them, his fat fingers get covered in red powder. I'm pretty sure he lives alone. His office is decorated with bullshit certificates that make him feel like he's accomplished something in life. He acts like the office is all his, but he actually shares it with the morning and night shift managers, who let him decorate as he pleases because they feel sorry for him. He's insecure about everything in his life, but he'll never admit it. He can't. He's the manager.

I pull into the Rudy's parking lot and park next to Henry's Calypso Thunder. The inside of his car is empty. I exit my LaPree and hurry toward the entrance.

The automatic glass doors open to reveal Gary leaning against a row of carts. "Tick tock," he says. I ignore him and search the aisles for Henry. Once these stupid group members see us together, they'll leave me alone. They're only after me because I don't belong to anything. People hate outsiders, and since I have no friends, I'm seen as a threat.

"Excuse me," says some customer with a camera strung around his neck. "Do you work here?"

"Yes," I say. "How can I help you?"

He tells me he's a photographer at Den's Lab and requires assistance in the meat section. This is why I need my sweatshirt. I'm not even clocked in yet, but if I refuse to help this guy and he complains, Pete will go berserk.

"You ready to work it, Tommy?" asks the photographer.

"Um . . . sure."

For the next half hour or so, I'm stuck holding up various steaks, pork chops, and trays of ground beef while this guy snaps photos. Supposedly he only eats meat that has the right *look*. I didn't ask him why he needs his meat to *look* so good. Customers never make any sense. They just like bothering employees because they can. Anyway, when the photo shoot finally ended, my plan to locate and isolate Henry before he met anyone else had been ruined, as the High School and College Kids had beaten me to him.

The Old Men, the Women's Circle, and the Voyeurs spend the afternoon talking amongst themselves. Whenever someone new gets hired, every employee seems to be on edge. Word on the grocery floor is that Henry's in with the High School and College Kids. War activity is postponed until further notice.

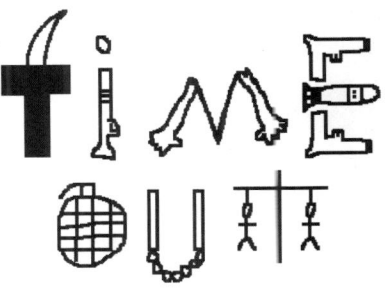

I use a box of Magic O's as a Face Blocker to spy on Henry. The High School and College Kids have yet to leave his side. I can only imagine what they're telling him.

"Tom's a loser."

"Tom's not twenty-six; he's thirty-six!"

"Tom watches *employees*."

I never should have lied to Henry about being super popular, but lying is what I do. I've been programmed to lie from working this horrible job. Most liars cheat and steal, too. That's how the phrase goes: you lie, you cheat, you steal. I only lie and steal. I'm sure I'd cheat if I had the opportunity, but I'm not in school, I don't have a girlfriend, and I rarely play board games.

⎕⎕⎕

Henry's sitting at the small plastic kitchen table we never use eating one of his micro meals when I enter the apartment.

"Where were you today?" he asks.

I take off my shoes and close the door. "What do you mean?"

"I didn't see you at work."

"Was today your first day?" I ask as I set my Night Burger bag on the wooden coffee table.

"Yeah," Henry says. "Didn't you get my note?"

I sit on the blue couch. "What note?"

"Do you have any friends at Rudy's?"

"What?"

"According to Ryan McGovern, you're that weird guy nobody talks to."

I reach into my Night Burger bag and shove a handful of Space Sticks into my mouth.

"So what do you have to say for yourself?"

"You jus met hese people," I mumble. "We've been friends over twenty years."

"Why would Ryan say something like that?"

"No idea." I pull out my burger. "Want half of this?"

"No."

The apartment gets quiet. Henry stares at me like he wants to kill me. I peel back the gold wrapper. "Mmm, these burgers—"

"Enough of that!" shouts Henry. "You work tomorrow?"

"Ah . . . yeah." I bite into the burger.

"Good. Tomorrow. Meeting in the condiment aisle. Five o'clock. Be there."

I swallow. "Sure."

I sneak a peek down the condiment aisle and see Henry and a bunch of High School and College Kids. I leave. No way am I walking into that. They'd all stare at me and be like, "This guy's a loser." I can lie about being popular in front of Henry but not in front of them. I don't do well in large groups. Whenever I'm around a lot of people, my mind shuts off. I can't comprehend anything and words become meaningless sounds. I've convinced myself numerous times that I'm suffering from some sort of mental disability. One of these days, I'm going to wake up and forget how to function. I won't be able to walk or talk or do anything. That's going to be a great day, because I doubt Henry will be around to feed me. I'll end up starving to death. That's a tough way to die. Not *tough* as in cool, but *tough* as in painful.

I catch up with Henry in the parking lot after work and explain how I got stuck helping customers and couldn't make the meeting.

"Bullshit."

"What?"

He opens his car door. "I've heard enough of your lies."

"But—"

"Just leave me alone, Tom."

"Fine!" I yell. "Let those STUPID High School and College Kids brainwash you! That's what they're doing! It's just like when the aliens do it!"

Henry enters his car and closes the door.

"We'll talk more at the apartment," I say as he reverses and drives off.

I've come to the realization that my plan involving Henry working at Rudy's so the three main groups would get off my back was the worst plan ever created. Not only is Henry now running with the High School and College Kids (which according to Gary, Raven, and Stan classifies him as an inactive war participant), but also, thanks to my alien brainwashing comment, we are no longer speaking. Henry doesn't even come home anymore. I only see him at work.

It's terrible. I'm basically watching my best friend make new friends and succeed in life. I don't want to watch that.

Rudy's is an all-out war zone. I've never seen so much chaos and destruction. Aisles destroyed. Fruit and vegetables smashed. *The deli!* You don't want to know what's happening in the deli! I can't believe there aren't any customer complaints. It's like the customers, Pete, and the High School and College Kids can't *see* the violence that's happening right in front of them. All three main groups warn me each day, "You better join soon or else." I wish I could quit Rudy's, but the idea of finding another job twists my stomach. It wouldn't matter much anyway, because every job's the same. A lot of people think that working some new job will make everything better, but that's never the case. You just have to face whatever you're facing and hope to get through it.

Henry bagged groceries for Lisa today. I've done that a few times, but I was always afraid to talk to her. Henry's not afraid to talk to anyone. Not only did he talk to Lisa, but he also made her laugh. Henry's not even funny. I don't think he's ever told a joke in his life. I'm not funny either, but if he's making her laugh, I can too. I need to buy the latest volume of *The Book of Jokes* and refresh myself on some material. "A man, a donkey, and a duck go swimming. Who drowns?" I'll tell Lisa that stuff and she'll think I'm hilarious. She'll dump Henry and then I'll become the Rudy's

All-Star. The stupid High School and College Kids will be like "Tell us that man, donkey, duck joke again." No more King Henry. All hail King Tom! It's going to be a sad day for Henry when his crown gets ripped off his head and placed on mine. He's going to need a lot of tissues to soak up his tears. Good thing I have a trunk full of stolen toilet paper. I can sell it to him. Ten bucks a roll. He owes me big for canceling the cable and treating me like this. He'll probably need therapy. I could have been a therapist if I wanted, but who wants to sit around and listen to crazies talk a bunch of nonsense?

"Thank you for calling Mr. Jim's Life Improvement Kit order placement center, Ms. Lydia speaking."

"Hi," I say over the phone. "I'd like to order the Life Improvement Kit."

"Yes, sir, and your name?"

"Mitchell. Tom Mitchell."

The refrigerator is still stocked with Henry's yogurt, micro meals, and other healthy selections. He's losing weight every day. It's like, whenever he loses a pound, he gains a friend. On Henry's days off, when I'm at work, he returns to the apartment and throws parties in my bedroom. There are always empty pizza boxes, smashed beer cans, and cigarette butts all over the carpet and on my air mattress. I wrote him a note requesting that he stop. He wrote back *HA HA HA!* I'm like one of those crazy scientists who gives life to monsters, except I didn't hook Henry up to any wires and shoot electricity into him. I shot false positivity into him. I need to find some angry men with torches. If only Henry went to Night Burger with me on his first day at Rudy's, like I had planned, none of this would have happened. I hate him. Well, I don't *hate* hate him, but I'm starting to develop something inside me that's like hate. I wish he were still my friend, but he doesn't want that anymore. *FUCK HIM!* That's exactly what I'm talking about. There's, like, some madness inside me that wants to come out. He doesn't care about me. He's only worried about getting popular and dating Lisa. He probably wants to become manager of Rudy's so he can control me at work, too. I don't like people who strive for much. Everyone should accept whatever situation they're given and deal with it. I'm going to work at a grocery store my whole life. It's fine. I've accepted it. People need to accept things. I should accept that Henry's no longer my friend, but I can't. Something inside me won't allow it.

eight

SMITH'S PARK was packed. A Glenshire police car blocked the main entrance. The red and blue lights flashed around and around. Two policemen stood in the middle of Davis Street holding flashlights and directing traffic. "Lot's full!" I heard one of them say as Henry and I pedaled past. Cars parked along the side of the street. People carried coolers, blankets, and lawn chairs. Little kids ran around laughing and holding sparklers. *BANG! BANG! BANG!* A bunch of firecrackers exploded.

"Forget the restaurant," I yelled to Henry. "We're going to miss the fireworks show."

"We'll be fine," Henry yelled back.

We biked away from the park and further up Davis Street. We still had a good five-minute ride until we reached the restaurant. It sat on the edge of Glenshire. Henry and I discovered it a few months back while it was being built. A lot of our free time was spent biking to the construction site and exploring the wooden skeleton. There was always garbage covering the gravel floor: empty pizza boxes, smashed beer cans, cigarette butts. Once the building started taking shape and Henry and I could no longer make our way inside, we stopped riding out that way. A sign posted outside the building read: *New Restaurant Opening July 4th.*

"You see that?!" Henry shouted.

There was a bright light ahead in the distance.

"Yeah!" I shouted back.

"Let's go!"

I watched Henry disappear into the darkness.

"Wait up!"

I shifted into a higher gear and struggled to pedal forward. I heard a clanking noise and started pedaling super fast. My chain fell off. "Henry!"

I jumped off my bike. The darkness made it difficult to see. A car blew past. *BEEP! BEEP! BEEP!* I grabbed the chain and pushed in the metal bar near the rear tire to give the chain slack. One, two, three more cars. I wrapped the chain around the spiky circle and spun the pedal with my hand to make sure the chain was on. I got back on my bike and pedaled as fast as I could.

"Henry!" I screamed. "HENRY!"

As I pedaled up Davis Street, night started turning into day. Henry was up ahead. His bike lay on the ground and he stood directly underneath this big round sign.

"HEY!" I rode up to him and dropped my bike on the pavement. "You shouldn't have left me back there."

Silence.

"Say something."

He lifted his arm and pointed at a gigantic moon with the words *Night Burger* glowing in yellow.

"It's brighter than the moon," Henry finally said.

I stared at the sign and replied, "I know."

From the outside, Night Burger looked like the future. The sign alone reminded me of some sort of alien signaling device. It was planted into the ground by a thick metal pole, and it lit up the night sky with a purpose. The building itself was shoebox-shaped and topped with a flat red roof. The outside brick was painted green and marked with colorful paintings that displayed cosmic environments with stars and various burger planets. The windows were clear round bubbles, like, the tops of flying-saucers. Orange, yellow, and blue lights shone from the rooftop and the ground, illuminating the entire building.

We parked our bikes and entered the restaurant through one of those circular push doors that you see in the movies. The inside was even cooler than the outside. The lighting was dimmed, and the entire ceiling looked like a black sky filled with millions of stars. Random sound effects—creaks, whispers, spring noises, meteor blasts, rocket boosters— played over the restaurant speakers in a slow, steady rhythm. The walls were covered with more images of deep space environments and faraway galaxies. Aliens, black holes, burger planets, supernovas, and other universe-related scenes were painted in great detail. The tables and chairs glowed an eerie blue, and small orange lights dangled from strings on the ceiling. The smell could be described in one word: otherworldly.

"Greetings, earthlings!" someone said. "Welcome to Night Burger!"

A pale-skinned teen stood behind the counter wearing a green hat and blue collared shirt with the Night Burger moon logo on it. He smiled and asked, "Can I get you two earthlings something to eat?"

Henry and I slowly approached the counter. It was a purplish color and had yellow flashing lights running along the outer edges.

"Hello," Henry said.

"Greetings!" The employee's name tag read *Daniel*. He had dark eyes and a long oval face "Would you like to try our famous Burger Classic meal?"

I looked up at the menu. The edges were neon orange and the food items were listed in dark red: Galaxy Sandwich, Orbit Rings, Space Sticks. Everything had weird names, even the drinks: Saturn Fizz, Orange Quest, The Mad Doctor.

Henry nudged me. "What are you getting?"

"I don't know," I said.

"Is this your first time?" Daniel asked.

Henry and I nodded.

"I highly recommend the Burger Classic meal."

"What is it?" asked Henry.

"It's our famous Night Burger with a medium order of Space Sticks and medium drink."

I nodded to Henry.

"Sure. Two of those," Henry said.

"Two Burger Classics." Daniel pressed some buttons on the cash register. "Anything else?"

We shook our heads.

"Will you be eating here or returning to your home planet?"

"Here."

Daniel set two empty white foam cups on the purple counter. "It's going to be six eighteen."

Henry reached into his pocket and pulled out the ten-dollar bill that his parents gave him for food.

"Thank you." Daniel took the money and completed the transaction. "Three eighty-two is your change, and here is your Mission Report."

```
                Night Burger
              25436 Davis Street
              Edge of Glenshire

            MISSION REPORT  #26

7/4/1984  9:02 PM              DINE-IN
-------------------------------------------
ITEM                      QTY   PRICE
-------------------------------------------
Burger Classic Meal        2    $5.98
-------------------------------------------

                    Human Fee    .20
                    TOTAL    $6.18
```

We filled our cups at the Fueling Station and sat at one of the back tables. I got a Saturn Fizz and Henry got something called The Missing Link.

"What does your pop taste like?" I asked.

"It's not good," he said. "I think it's diet."

"This Saturn Fizz is great." I took a sip from the straw. "It's like drinking a strawberry sucker."

"Can I try it?"

"Sure."

I slid the pop across the blue table. Henry took a sip. "Very good."

My eyes drifted to the corner wall. There was a painting of a group of pink alien women holding hands in a circle, and in the middle of the circle was a lone spaceman.

"Hey," I whispered to Henry. "Do you think aliens exist?"

"Mission twenty-six!" a voice announced.

Henry reached into his pocket and pulled out his Mission Report. "That's us!"

Henry returned carrying a large red tray with two huge burgers wrapped in gold paper and two silver boxes of Space Sticks, which turned out to be fries.

"This looks amazing," I said.

Henry was already unwrapping his burger. "I'm starving." He shoved a handful of Space Sticks into his mouth.

I grabbed my burger off the tray. Just as I was about to unwrap it, I heard a loud bang. The few other earthlings who were eating in the dining room packed up and rushed out.

"The fireworks," I said.

Henry held his burger in his hands. "Oh well."

"You don't want to go?" I asked.

"I think this is cooler." He took his first bite.

I looked around and absorbed the colorful lights and random sound effects and cosmic images of Night Burger.

"You're right," I said. "This is cooler."

"Wow!" Henry exclaimed. "This burger is the best!"

BANG! BANG! BANG!

It sounded like there was a war going on outside. Thankfully, Henry and I had Night Burger to protect us. *BANG!* The outside forces were drawing near. *BANG! BANG!* Soon the war would be upon us. *BANG! BANG! BANG!*

I quickly unwrapped my burger and held it in my hands. This could be my last meal. I took a big bite.

"Mmm!" I said. "These burgers *are* the best!"

nine

ONE OF THE OLD MEN had a sudden heart attack and died today. I doubt it was really a heart attack. Somebody killed this old man. Time of death was approximately 5:43 p.m. The paramedics came in and took his body away on a stretcher. They wheeled him out through the entrance doors. Some nosy customer standing in the checkout line shouted, "Hey! Those men didn't pay for that!"

Pete made an announcement over the store intercom. Everyone looked up toward the ceiling during his speech. He barely said anything about the dead old guy; he just apologized to the customers for any inconvenience.

Stan informed me that the man who died was Bob Billings. Apparently, he and Bob were fishing buddies. I stood in silence next to my Jukebox Chicken stock while Stan proceeded to cry. I never know what to say to people who lose people they love. *Sorry Bob is dead, but I have my own problems to deal with.* That's the truth of the situation. I wish there were something I could do to make things better, but there's not. A lot of people claim that when you die, you go to a better place. If that's the case, I don't know why people get so upset over death. Bob's probably out fishing on a boat right now. When he was alive, he was working at Rudy's, but now that he's dead, he's out fishing on a boat. Sounds good to me.

Night Burger is falling apart. The giant moon is only half lit, and the yellow *N* in Night and two *r*'s and the *e* in Burger are burnt out. The sign reads *ight Bu g* . I told one of the employees about it, but they didn't seem to care. No one cares. The entire restaurant is going downhill. All the outside wall paintings are fading. The orange, yellow, and blue outdoor lights are burnt out. Even the food doesn't taste as good as it used to.

Henry still throws parties in my bedroom on his days off. I collect all the pizza boxes, beer cans, and cigarette butts in a big trash bag. I feel like one of those garbage-collecting prisoners you see on the side of the highway. It's not good to feel like a prisoner when you're not a prisoner, because you start acting like a prisoner. The other day, I made a shank out of my toothbrush. I don't even remember doing it, but the bottom end of my toothbrush is like a dagger now. *STAB! STAB!* I'm jealous of my apartment-mate and want him dead. He has a lot more freedom than I do. He also has friends and places to go. I don't have any of that. I'm going to be that old man walking alone up and down the street. Nowhere to go, no one to see. There are people in this world who are meant to be alone. They can't be around other people, can't make friends, and can't function in society. I'm beginning to think I'm one of those people.

Word on the grocery floor is that the Voyeurs are responsible for killing Bob, but another word on the grocery floor claims that the Women's Circle, angry over a recent voyeur sneak attack that led to the hospitalization of two women, Pat Markowitz and Sandy Vennings, made up that first word in order to pit the Old Men against the Voyeurs. No official statement has been made by the Old Men as they don't have the best of hearing and may not have even heard the first word, let alone the second. Either way, the death of Bob Billings has elevated the war to a whole new level.

The Voyeurs are focused on breaking legs. They got the idea from Legs, a voyeur who watches only legs. Supposedly, it's a proven fact that people, while standing, rarely look at their legs. Since legs are needed to work at Rudy's, the Voyeurs figure, take out the legs, take out the employee.

Raven, feeling responsible for Pat and Sandy's recent hospitalization, used a big chunk of the Women's saved-up overcharge money to purchase all types of weapons and armor. Each woman is now equipped with a bulletproof vest, a Taser gun, and a can of mace.

The Old Men beefed up their back room security and now have some tall, muscular, stone-faced guy guarding the door with old, frail Stan. Whenever I get my stock or take out the trash, the giant stares at me and cracks his knuckles.

Henry and the High School and College Kids are still oblivious. Pete and the customers are oblivious too. I don't understand why I can see the destruction but they can't. The three main groups are now threatening me with physical violence. They tell me I must join a side soon or prepare my body for excruciating pain.

I drive to Henry's mom's house on my day off. She still lives off Circle Trail in the same brown house with the curved driveway. I haven't been there in years. I'm not sure if it will work, but what I'm thinking is that if I can borrow Henry's old BMX from his mom and bring it to him, he might want to be friends again. Sometimes people need to *see* objects from their past to remind them of who they are. Right now, it's like Henry doesn't remember that we were ever friends. Not that I care about being friends with a backstabbing, girlfriend-stealing, *look how healthy and adult I am* Henry, but the bills are starting to pile up and considering the recent threats of violence against me, I could really use his muscle.

Henry's mom answers the front door wearing a cheetah-fur coat and squirrel mittens. I never thought that combination would work, but it looks pretty good.

"Hello, Mrs. Zanta," I say.

"Tom," she says. "Is that you?"

"Yes."

"It's been forever!" She gives me a hug. Her blonde hair smells like the zoo. "Come inside, my dear."

The house is decorated in various animal furs. The walls and ceiling are covered in giraffe. The carpet is made out of raccoon. The couches are all hyena.

"Don't you love what I've done to the place?" she asks.

"Looks good," I say.

"Looks *great*," she replies.

She grabs my arm and takes me on a house tour. We start in the living room, where she describes all the different furs: polar bear rug, prairie dog footrest, alpaca pillows. The next stop is the master bedroom, where she talks on and on about her lion bedspread.

"Whenever I sleep, I feel like the queen of the jungle."

If I had a lion bedspread, I could be *king* of the jungle. "How much do those bedspreads cost?" I ask.

"You couldn't afford it." Henry's mom points her squirrel hand toward the door. "Shall we?"

Every room is decorated: the buffalo bathroom, the kangaroo kitchen, the rare hairy-nosed wombat laundry room.

The house tour finally ends back in the living room where it started.

"It's all very nice," I say.

Henry's mom smiles and sits on her hyena couch. "You really think so?"

"Sure."

I think Henry's mom has a serious problem. It probably all started with that rabbit's foot she used to carry around when Henry and I were kids. I wouldn't doubt if she had something to do with Henry's dad blowing up in that car.

"So how's my Henry doing?" she asks.

"That's actually what I came here to talk to you about."

I sit in my LaPree and listen to talk radio. My car stereo doesn't play music stations so I'm forced to listen to talk. All talk show hosts ever talk about is news. I think people talk too much about news. No one has anything else to talk about. If I had a talk radio show, I'd probably end up talking about news too, because that's what everyone else is doing and if I'm not doing what everyone else is doing, people will hate me.

Shortly after 11 p.m., I spot Henry walking across the Rudy's parking lot. I grab the tiny BMX out of my trunk and roll it toward him.

"Surprise!" I yell.

Henry freezes. "Where'd you get that?"

"I picked it up from your mom's house."

"You went to my mom's house?"

"Yeah."

"Are you insane?"

"No."

"I haven't talked to my mom in years."

"I know," I say. "She says hi."

Henry looks out toward Davis Street and shakes his head. The overhead parking light flickers on and off. I roll the bike closer. "So how about a ride?"

Henry backs away. "Get that away from me."

"Why?" I ask.

"Because I have no interest in riding that thing."

"Why?" I ask again.

"Because I'm not a kid anymore."

"You don't have to be a kid to ride a bike."

"That's a kid's bike, Tom! In case you haven't noticed, I'm an adult!"

"We hate adults," I say.

"*You* hate adults!"

Henry storms over to his Calypso Thunder and opens the door.

"Where are you going?" I ask.

"Away from you."

Thankfully, Mr. Jim's Life Improvement Kit is sitting in the mail room when I return to the apartment. I take it upstairs and open the box to find a video and white T-shirt with the words **Don't Think** in bold, black lettering. I put the T-shirt on and pop the tape into the VCR. The screen displays Mr. Jim sitting on a chair made of money and smoking a cigar. There are two beautiful women on each side of him.

"Look at me!" he exclaims. "I have a great life! Want to know my secrets?"

"YES!" I shout.

Mr. Jim explains how the key to living a great life starts with making a mental list of all your problems (*Henry, Rudy's, the Old Men, the Women's Circle, the Voyeurs, Pete, Lisa, customers*) and erasing them from your mind.

"The most important skill a person must develop in order to live a great life is the skill of *not* thinking."

The video cuts to various real-life interviews about how thoughts lead to pain and worry and confusion.

- Interview one: Inadequate guy
- Interview two: Ugly girl
- Interview three: Montage of broken hearts

To avoid this pain, worry, and confusion, Mr. Jim recommends a series of exercises specifically designed to help those who are suffering. "Do these exercises whenever your brain wants to think, and you will go from thought*ful* to thought*less* in under a day."

To further help shut your brain off, Mr. Jim suggests wearing the **Don't Think** T-shirt as much as possible. "Wear the shirt to sleep, to work, out to parties." Wearing it to sleep is fine, but I don't know about work and parties. I don't go to parties, and there's absolutely no way Pete would allow me to wear—I cut myself off and do five Don't Think Push-ups.

"Don't think. Don't think. Don't think. Don't think. Don't think."

I turn off the TV and VCR and go to bed.

ten

"**I** WILL CONTROL the Burger Galaxy!"

"Not today, Burger Prince!" I yelled. "Commander Henry!"

"Yes, Commander Tom."

"Hit the Burger Prince with the Meteor Wave."

"You got it!"

Boom! Swoosh! Whirl!

"Aaaaah! Nooooooooo!" yelled the Burger Prince as the Meteor Wave blasted him into the Sea of Pickles. "I'll be baaaaaaaaaack!"

We sat at the glowing blue table and congratulated each other on another victory.

"Good work, Commander Tom."

"You too, Commander Henry."

Once again, we had defeated the evil Burger Prince and saved the Burger Galaxy from his tyrannical rule. All of our alien friends rejoiced and thanked us for keeping them safe.

The Burger Galaxy consisted of all the planets, stars, and aliens painted on the Night Burger interior walls. For the most part, it was a friendly and peaceful galaxy; however, one alien, known as the Burger Prince, hated everything about it. He was a tall, skinny alien with a gold crown and a sly smirk. Ever since his royal parents died in a spaceship accident, he'd been using his royal power for evil rather than good. His master plan, One Mind, was based off the idea of *control* in that he wanted everyone to think like him, do whatever he said, and worship the space ground he walked on. Henry and I defeated the Burger Prince over many Burger Classic meals, but he was one of those evil villains who always came back for more.

When we weren't busy saving the Burger Galaxy from complete destruction, Henry and I used our All-Access Heroes Travel Card to explore the various burger planets. Tundle had giant fly-like bugs that the aliens drove as cars. Vorus was known for its never-ending waterfalls and aquatic residents. Pon spun around and around and felt like living on a giant treadmill. Kalmax, our alien guide and biggest fan, dressed in flashy suits and had tentacles coming out of his head. The first planet he took us to was his home planet of Zoot. It was an upside-down planet where everyone walked upside down. Kalmax showed us the meteor hut where he grew up, introduced us to his three best friends (Jeggs, Brint, and Tizzy), took us out for dinner at the galaxy-famous Terrestrial Crossing, and even brought us to the Ding Lounge to watch his brother's rock band play.

Night Burger sped up time and took us on thousands of super galactic adventures. Whenever we passed through the circular push doors, our imaginations went wild. Oftentimes, we would get so lost in pretending that we were space commanders, called to duty by the giant moon to protect the

Burger Galaxy from the Burger Prince, that we forgot we were ordinary kids and had to do ordinary kid things like go to school, do homework, eat dinner with our parents, clean our rooms, take showers, brush our teeth, and sleep.

The invasion started the summer before Henry and I entered junior high. One kid. Two kids. Three kids. Before we knew it, everyone knew about Night Burger.

I confronted Henry and asked him if he broke the promise we made after our first visit to keep Night Burger a secret.

"I didn't tell anyone," he pleaded. "I swear."

He was lying. I'd seen him talking to other kids in school. I never talked to anyone. I only spoke when absolutely necessary, like when we worked in groups or when the teacher called on me to answer a question. Talking was too dangerous. I knew that if other kids found out about Night Burger, the entire Burger Galaxy would be in jeopardy.

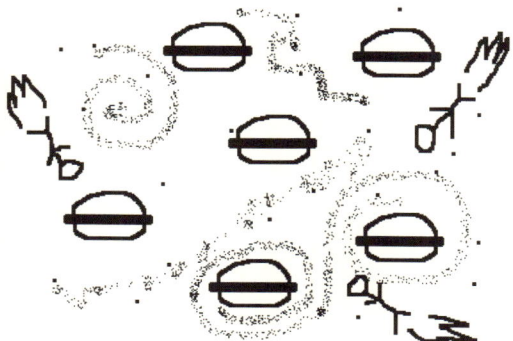

Lines started to form at Night Burger, and the glowing blue tables began filling up with rambunctious kids whose loud voices muffled the random sound effects and ruined our ability to imagine. The Fueling Station was constantly occupied. The wall paintings smeared with greasy fingerprints. The tile floor littered with empty burger wrappers and half-eaten Space Sticks. Night Burger was being attacked. The Burger Prince was growing in strength. He absorbed the chaotic energy from the rowdy crowd and used his newfound power to control alien minds all throughout the Burger Galaxy. Eyes wide, Henry and I stood back in horror as our hopes and dreams were crushed by a group of loud, annoying, and disrespectful beings known as humans.

A new war had begun. The only thing left to do was fight. All intruders were classified as enemies and must be destroyed.

"Listen up, commander," I said to Henry.

He set his burger on the red tray and finished chewing. "Yeah."

"We should challenge that group of kids over there to a race down Davis Street," I said. "Losers leave Night Burger for good."

Henry looked over his shoulder. The kids were sitting three booths down and throwing pickles at the wall painting of Kalmax. "I don't know."

"Come on," I pleaded. "We need to protect Kalmax and defeat the Burger Prince and save the Burger Galaxy."

"They're not doing anything." Henry went back to eating his burger.

I couldn't believe him. Those kids were doing something. They were part of the infestation responsible for destroying the Night Burger we knew and loved. The *only* kids that should even be allowed inside Night Burger were me and Henry. We were the ones who discovered Night Burger. We used to hang out here before it even opened, back when it was just some wooden skeleton. As far as I was concerned, Night Burger was ours! All ours!

eleven

THE GARAGE DOOR opens. Henry's mom stands next to
her purple Tulip Convertible. She has her bunny slippers on.

"Did you tell my Henry I miss him?" she asks.

"Yeah," I say as I lean the tiny BMX against the tiger
wall.

"He hasn't called."

"I'm sure he'll call soon." I exit the garage and walk
back to my car. "Thanks for letting me borrow the bike."

"Wait!" Henry's mom calls out. "Come inside and feel
my new panda tablecloth."

"I can't."

"Why not?"

Quick-Response Sit-up. "I'm allergic."

"Nonsense," she says. "No one's allergic to panda."

I do an Escape Jumping Jack and make up some lie
about visiting a panda petting zoo and sneezing like crazy.

"My eyes were watering and everything," I say.

She calls me a *liar* and warns that I am no longer allowed on her property unless I have a doctor's note saying that I'm, in fact, allergic to panda.

"You even think about showing up here without a note, and I'll call the police!" she screams as I enter my LaPree.

The Rudy's parking lot is packed. It's like this every Saturday. Sundays, too. I drive up and down the rows and rows of cars until I find a spot. I'm going to have to bag groceries once inside. I don't mind bagging. The worst part is the paper bags. If you're a customer who asks for paper bags, please kill yourself. Also, if you're a customer who asks for double-bagged paper bags, please kill yourself and your entire family. There's no need for double paper! There's no need for any paper! *Relaxation Neck Roll.* I'm just saying that plastic is fine. The only reason we still offer paper is that customers will freak if paper isn't around.

"You don't have paper?!" I can imagine some customer saying. "I can't live without paper!"

I hate how customers get whatever they want. *Brainless Breathing.* Inhale/Exhale. They need to accept the fact that not everything's going to be exactly the way they imagine. I blame businesses for ingraining this sort of superior mindset into customers. *Emergency Elbow Bends.* I get that they want their customers to be happy, but it has gone way beyond that. Employees aren't even allowed to be human anymore. We are robots, programmed by our employers to smile and obey each and every customer command. *Yes, sir. Yes, ma'am. Thank you. Have a nice day.*

All ten registers are open. There are customers everywhere: walking around, pushing carts, standing in line, talking to employees. In order to reach the time clock without any impromptu meat photo shoots or other interruptions, I walk fast and do my best to avoid customers who look like they have questions. If you don't know how to tell when a customer's about to ask a question, here are the three main warning signs:

1. The Head Scratch

A customer who scratches his or her head is ninety-five percent likely to ask a question. Many people think I got this first warning sign from watching too many cartoons, but it's true.

2. Reading Labels

Any customer who spends time reading labels is an automatic pain and true question-asker. These customers love asking questions about calories and ingredients and whatnot. I hate these customers because they assume that the employees know *every* detail about *every* product.

3. The Lost Look

This is very easy to understand. Basically, if a customer's looking around like they're lost, get the hell out of there as fast as possible because they're about to ask a question.

I safely reach the time clock and punch in my four-digit employee code. As soon as I push the Clock In button, the office door flies open.

"Get in here, Mitchell!"

I enter Pete's office. He grabs a bag of Zolo's Chips off his desk and starts popping them into his mouth. I don't like staring at people while they eat, so I look away.

"Can't even look me in the eyes, huh?"

"What?"

Pete gets right up in my face. I can smell Captain Zolo's fire sauce on his breath. "You stealing candy, Mitchell?"

"No."

Pete tosses the bag of chips across the office and licks his red powdered fingers clean.

"I believe this belongs to you," he says as he opens the bottom file drawer and pulls out my gray sweatshirt.

"My sweatshirt!" I say. "Where'd you find it?"

"Guilty!" Pete screams. "Found it in the break room. The pockets were loaded with Zook bars, Tops Taffy, Fruity Tooties—you name it!"

"That's strange."

"Strange, my foot!" Pete yells. "You're stealing candy!"

"I didn't take that stuff," I say. "My sweatshirt's been missing for over a month."

"I see, the old missing sweatshirt excuse," Pete says. "If your sweatshirt's been missing, why haven't I seen any Missing Sweatshirt posters hanging around?"

"I planned on making some, but—"

"Tell it to the judge!"

"What?"

"Shut up!" Pete shouts. "Listen, you're lucky I like ya, Mitchell, but hear this: I'm onto ya, and if I find out you're thieving in my store, I'll fly ya outta here faster than a kite in a windstorm."

Pete throws my sweatshirt at me. "Now get up front and start bagging!"

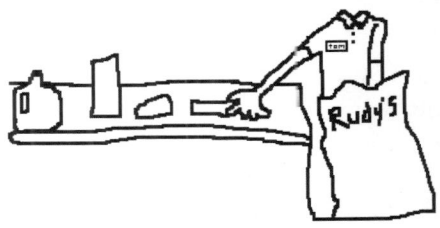

Someone set me up. *Don't Think Push-up.* But who? *No-Thought Crunch.* Or why? *Leave-My-Brain Leg Bend.* Henry! I'll kill him! Wait, no, it can't be. My sweatshirt was missing before he started. It had to be those two women who were torturing that old man awhile back in the break room sink. Or maybe it was the old man. I don't think it was the Voyeurs. And I doubt it was the High School and College Kids. They would never touch my sweatshirt. I'm like a disease to them. Henry's mom has a disease. Thanks to Mr. Jim's Escape Jumping Jack, she now thinks I'm allergic to panda. These stupid exercises aren't working. I'm jealous of people who can turn off their minds. I'm always thinking about something. Sometimes, my thoughts don't make any sense. I create things that don't exist. I have experiences I've never experienced. The reality is that I don't have any control. My life has been taken over by this job and Henry and customers and the three main employee groups. I sometimes get scared at night, because when I'm lying on my air mattress and looking into the darkness, I think about how I've never had and may never have control, and the twisted thought slips into my head that maybe I would like to become a Rudy's manager one day, but now that will never happen because Pete thinks I'm a candy thief. I really wish I could *not* think, but it's impossible. There's always something to think about. Not thinking only delays everything and makes things worse. I should have known Mr. Jim was a crook from that toupee he was wearing. It's like, if he's hiding the fact that he's bald, what else is he hiding?

I pull some customer's empty shopping cart toward the bagging area and await his groceries.

"I take Vitamin C at least once a day," Judy says as she scans a bag of Let's Be Healthy Vitamin C Drops.

"Same here," says the tan and muscular customer. "We must have the same doctor."

They both laugh.

Judy's the interrogation specialist for the Women's Circle. She's got bright red hair, piercing green eyes, and huge breasts. I can't stand bagging for her because she loves to talk. All it does is hold up the line. If I were her customer, I'd be like, "Don't talk to me." Well, I wouldn't say that, but I'd be thinking it. This guy doesn't seem to mind the talking. A lot of people actually like talking to people they don't know. It makes no sense.

Judy's now calling the customer Gus, and they're having a friendly debate over which brand of pickles is the best.

"Halmax Pickles are the crunchiest," Gus says.

"Yes, I agree," Judy replies, "but Decan's have a much *sweeter* flavor."

I could never talk pickles with some random customer. The only person I could talk pickles with is Henry, but since we're not talking, I can't talk pickles with anyone. Not that I'm dying for some pickle talk, but the point I'm trying to make is that I have no one to talk to. The only person besides Henry who I'm interested in talking with is Lisa, but that's not going to happen. You need friends to talk to girls like Lisa. I can't walk up to her and be like, "Hey, I'm Tom Mitchell. Yes, I know, dumb name. Anyway, I work here and have no friends." She'd want nothing to do with me. If Henry didn't betray me, Lisa and I would probably be dating. Girlfriends are good because they help you forget your friends, or friend. I know this from dating Cassie. Oftentimes I imagine Henry and Lisa together—kissing, holding hands, laughing. It drives me crazy and keeps me up at night. I've tried tricking my brain into thinking that Lisa secretly likes me, but my brain is not falling for it. "Lisa will never secretly like you, Tom," my brain tells me. "If she had any idea what was going on inside your mind, she'd think you're crazy and hit you with her purse or something." Oh well. At least I have my sweatshirt back.

"Hold it!" says Gus. "I wanted paper."

Everything's already bagged and sitting in his cart. He should have told me he wanted paper earlier instead of talking to Judy about pickles and Vitamin C and all that other crap.

"Oh, sorry." I practice my Brainless Breathing (Inhale/Exhale) while removing the plastic bags from the cart.

"On second thought"—Gus winks at Judy—"make it double paper."

twelve

SHORTLY AFTER entering junior high, Henry joined the
football team. He didn't tell me until afterward.

"You should have told me you were thinking about joining."

"Why?" Henry asked.

"Because it's important."

I'm sure he was pressured into joining by the coaches.
They prowled the hallways between class periods searching
for athletic kids and forcing them to play sports. Henry grew
to almost six feet over the summer. I didn't grow at all. The
coaches walked right past me.

Henry practiced every Monday, Wednesday, Friday, and Saturday. Games every Sunday. Friday and Saturday night sleepovers were canceled. We only hung out on Tuesdays and Thursdays. Football made Henry tired and lazy. All we did anymore was sit inside and watch TV. We didn't even go to Night Burger. I wanted to remind him that we had a responsibility to protect the Burger Galaxy from the Burger Prince, but all that stuff sounded kind of stupid now that we were in the seventh grade.

Junior high was a lot different from elementary school. All the kids were trying to act way more important and cooler than they actually were. Cartoons, bikes, toys, and everything we loved as kids was now dumb. Everyone rushed to make friends and separated into groups: jocks, nerds, druggies. Henry belonged to the jocks because he played football. I didn't belong to anything, which annoyed members of various groups and led to several hallway and bathroom confrontations.

"Who do you run with?"

"I'm friends with Henry Zanta."

"So you're a jock?"

"Not really."

"Then what are you?"

i am nothing

Eventually, the groups became so angry at my lack of affiliation that they began threatening to kick my ass if I didn't join something.

I informed Henry of the threats one Tuesday night during a TV commercial.

"What are their names?" he asked.

I sat on his bedroom floor and wrote out a list: Stu Hebert, Gerald Manhour, Ray Jacobson.

"That all of them?"

"Yes."

Henry must have gone after them and straightened things out, because from that moment on, the groups stopped bothering me.

For Henry's thirteenth birthday, he invited me over for a Friday night sleepover. I got to his house a little after 6 p.m. His mom answered the door.

"Come in, Tom," she said. "Henry's in his bedroom."

I took off my shoes and walked down the long hallway to Henry's room. He was still in his football gear and removing all his E-Z-Rest pictures from the walls.

"What are you doing?" I asked.

"Taking these down," he replied.

"Why?"

"I just don't want them up."

I found out why Henry took down the E-Z-Rest pictures when the doorbell rang and there stood his new football friends: Tony Fuller, Rob Markers, Erik Heapers, and Mike Milroy. It was the first birthday party where Henry had invited other kids. They all brought cool sleeping bags and showered him with awesome gifts: Tornado football, *Warzone Apocalypse 2* handheld video game, *Greatest Football Moments* VHS tape, Electronix boom box. I didn't even own a sleeping bag, and all I gave Henry was a package of these capsules that transform into foam dinosaurs when you put them in water.

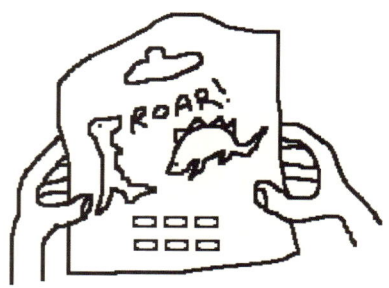

The best gift was from Henry's parents. A brand new GoMax mountain bike. My head almost exploded when his dad rolled it into the living room. It was blue with black handgrips and had twenty speeds, off-road tires, and a plastic water bottle connected to the frame. I could tell by the look on Henry's face that he wasn't happy. He didn't want a new bike. He wanted an E-Z-Rest.

Henry's dad ordered two giant pepperoni pizzas from Big Topping Pizza. I ate in silence as Tony, Rob, Erik, Mike, and Henry talked about football and how they needed to win on Sunday to make the playoffs.

"We have to win."

"We must win."

"We need to win."

As soon as we finished eating, we headed to Henry's bedroom to play *Warzone Apocalypse 2*. The game was only one player, so whenever someone was killed in battle, we switched turns. I was by far the best virtual soldier and killed everything that moved.

"You got some serious skills, Mitchell," Erik said.

"Thanks."

The whole time I was playing, I was imagining blowing away Tony, Rob, Erik, and Mike.

Around midnight, the guys started rolling out their cool sleeping bags. They were still talking football.

"You can't even catch a cold, Heapers," said Tony.

"I caught that winning touchdown pass against the Bandits," Erik said. "Milroy's the butterfingers."

"The sun got in my eyes," Mike replied.

"Get a room, ladies!" Rob groaned.

They all laughed.

Henry turned off the TV and crawled into his bed. He used to sleep in a red race car bed, but due to his growth spurt, he now had a normal one. I walked over to the closet to grab my go-to blanket and pillow.

"This was a good time, Zanta," said Rob.

"Yeah, Zanta, good work."

"Cool party."

"What Fuller said."

"Thanks, guys, I'm glad you all came," Henry replied.

I dropped my go-to blanket and pillow on the floor next to the closet. I typically sleep next to Henry's bed but the guys were all sprawled out around it. Just as I was about to lie down, a voice called out, "Hey, Mitchell. Hit those lights."

😑 😑 😑

"The guys think you're all right," Henry told me at the bus stop Monday morning.

"I don't have much in common with them," I said.

"Just give it some time," Henry replied. "Oh, and guess what?"

"What?"

"We made the playoffs!"

≣ ≣ ≣

When football season finally ended, I thought things would go back to normal, but no. Henry continued to talk and hang out with his new football friends. He even convinced me to move lunch tables. We used to eat lunch with Fritz Parks, Ken Tribe, and Ed Domski. They were all super quiet and didn't even talk to one another. I loved it. Now we ate with Heapers, Fuller, Markers, Milroy, and a whole bunch of other loud last-name jocks who constantly talked about sports. It was horrible. Everything was horrible. I couldn't stand junior high. There was more homework, no recess, and the students and teachers were all jerks. I got an after-school detention once for questioning my English teacher, Mrs. Wells, about a non-fiction narrative essay I wrote about riding bikes. I put in there how bikes went faster at night and she disagreed. She wrote on my paper *This is a NON-FICTION essay, not FICTION* and gave me a C. I spoke to her after class and told her she didn't know what she was talking about. She said I had a behavior problem and sent me to Principal Lutter's office.

The summer came and went. Henry and I got to hang out a little more, but it wasn't like it used to be. He spent a lot of time playing backyard football with his new friends. Every now and again, he invited me to tag along, but I was never interested. Instead, I rode my ten-speed around Glenshire, visiting the old hot spots—The Big Hill, Smith's Park, The Fields. Whenever I got bored, I'd pretend Henry was with me.

"Let's ride to The Long Trail!"

"Yeah, Tom!"

Pretend Henry always did whatever I wanted. He was nothing like real Henry. Real Henry was boring and only wanted to hang out with his football friends and watch TV.

"How come you never want to go to Night Burger anymore?" I asked real Henry one night.

"Well, to get to Night Burger, I would need a bike."

"You have a brand new GoMax sitting in your garage."

"I already told you, I'm not riding that thing."

"Because of the E-Z-Rest?"

"Yeah," Henry said. "I've been asking for that recliner since I was five. Any gift my parents give me that isn't an E-Z-Rest is *not* wanted."

"What about your BMX?" I asked.

"No way," Henry replied. "I'm way too big."

On the final day of summer, I biked to Night Burger alone. It was packed with human intruders. I purchased my Burger Classic meal with money my parents had paid me for cleaning and helping out around the house. I ate in the back corner. After I finished my food, I sat and stared at the wall paintings and remembered all the fun Henry and I used to have traveling to the various planets, hanging out with the different aliens, and keeping the Burger Galaxy safe. Some idiot drew mustaches on a bunch of the aliens, which made no sense because, according to Kalmax, aliens couldn't grow facial hair.

Eighth grade was worse than seventh. Henry joined football again and practiced not four but five days a week: Monday, Wednesday, Thursday, Friday, and Saturday. Games every Sunday. Friday and Saturday night sleepovers were once again canceled. The only day we hung out was Tuesday. Henry was now tape recording E-Z-Rest commercials off the TV and never wanted to leave his room. My life was boring. I basically went to school and came straight home. I didn't feel like riding my bike, going to Night Burger, or doing anything. My mom wasn't too happy.

"He just mopes around all day," I heard her complain to my dad.

"He's a teenager."

"We should return him."

"We're not returning him."

≧ ≧ ≧

"Hopefully your parents get you that E-Z-Rest because, eventually, you're not going to be able to walk," I told Henry one Tuesday night.

He paused the E-Z-Rest commercial he was watching and asked, "What are you talking about?"

"That's what football does to you," I said. "It destroys your body and makes your bones hurt."

"That's a lie."

"It's true. Take a look at this picture."

I handed Henry a photo of this messed-up-looking drug addict I had cut out of my health textbook.

"What's wrong with his face?" he asked.

"I guess football destroys your face, too."

On the Friday before the big Homecoming game, Henry announced to the lunch table that he was going to give his football jersey to Cindy VonBeck.

"Get outta here, Zanta!" shouted Heapers.

"Cindy V's the most popular girl in school," said Milroy.

Henry stood up and walked three tables over. We watched in silence as Cindy V accepted the jersey by giving Henry a hug and kiss on the cheek. The entire school made a huge deal over it.

"Did you hear that Zanta gave his jersey to Cindy V?"

"This is BIG!"

Henry was moving past me on all levels. He was making new friends, meeting girls, and becoming a part of something. It didn't make sense why he was one way and I was another. We grew up together and lived similar lives. We should be the same. Henry's great at making friends. I'm horrible at making friends. Even if I wanted to make friends, I couldn't. Talking to strangers freezes me up. Henry should have recognized this about me and kept by my side, but he didn't. He joined the football team and, after that jersey exchange, became King of Glenshire Junior High School.

For Henry's fourteenth birthday, he invited me to another sleepover party. I called him the night of and told him I was sick.

"That sucks," he said.

"Yeah." Fake cough. "Wish I could make it."

I rode to Night Burger that night. It was pretty cold outside, but I needed to get out and do something. The inside was packed with all sorts of unfamiliar faces. All I could see was different shapes and colors. Strange voices echoed over the random sound effects. I ordered my Burger Classic meal and stood by the Fueling Station until my mission number was called.

"Mission sixty-two!"

The employee verified my Mission Report and handed me my red food tray. "Thanks."

I sat at the back table, away from everyone else. I didn't look at the wall paintings or imagine anything. I just sat with my head down and ate my food.

"Hey," a voice said halfway through my meal.

I looked up and saw Henry. "Hey."

"I thought you were sick," he said.

"I was, but it went away."

"That was fast."

"Yeah." I ate a Space Stick. "What are you doing here?"

"My dad drove us up here to eat," he said. "We're sitting by the Burger Prince."

There was a whole group of them. They were all wearing their stupid football jerseys. I recognized Heapers and Milroy.

"You told them about Night Burger?" I asked.

"Yeah, they've never been here before."

"You weren't supposed to tell anyone."

"Why?" Henry asked.

"Because we promised not to."

"I didn't think we were still doing that."

"Who else did you tell?"

"No one."

"Yeah, right." My eyes scanned the dining room. "Then how did all these *intruders* find out about this place?"

"I don't know."

"You told them, didn't you?!"

"I didn't tell anyone."

I sipped my Saturn Fizz and said nothing.

"Look, I gotta get back," Henry said. "You wanna come sit by us?"

I shook my head. "I think my cold returned." Fake cough. Fake cough.

Henry walked over to his friends. They welcomed him back with high fives and laughs. I sat alone under the starlit ceiling, staring at my food. The Burger Prince had won. *Sorry, Kalmax, but Henry and I are no longer space commanders and can no longer protect the Burger Galaxy from complete destruction.* I started to feel sick. I got up from the table and left.

thirteen

I'M STEALING toilet paper again. Whenever I'm called out to gather carts, the first thing I do is head to the break room and grab my gray sweatshirt (which I now keep secured in a break room locker). Once I'm zipped up, I enter the employee bathroom, find an empty stall, and stick a toilet paper roll down my pants. My sweatshirt conceals the evidence perfectly and allows me to exit the store no problem. I keep the rolls in my car trunk. My collection is quite impressive. I'm sure that if I showed it to those stupid High School and College Kids, they'd be like, "Wow, you're awesome!"

Pete still thinks I'm a candy thief. He set up a surveillance tent in the candy aisle. Turns out him finding my sweatshirt was a good thing. It's good to have a fake crime covering up the real crime. Right now, Pete's thinking *candy* when he should be thinking *toilet paper*. I don't even like candy. The only reason I would steal candy is to sell it, but it's not worth the trouble. The main buyers of candy are kids. I can't sell candy to kids. People would think I'm up to no good. "Why is that man selling kids candy?" I don't like calling myself a man, but I'm twenty-six years old. I can't call myself a kid anymore. I'm a man. I have to face it. I don't want to. I don't feel like a man. I don't have a wife or kids. I don't own a house. I don't even have a real job. Well, I have a real job, but I hate it. Men are supposed to take pride in their work. I don't take pride in anything at Rudy's. I'm not a man. A man tells things how he sees them. I don't tell anyone anything. I keep my mouth shut and let things boil up inside until I can't take it anymore. I hate small talk. I hate customers. I hate pretty much everything. A man doesn't let the little things bother him. I can't even say the word man without feeling uncomfortable. "Man." Chills, panic, anxiety. If I were locked in a room and someone repeated *man, man, man . . .* I'd lose my mind. People lose their minds over all sorts of things—illnesses, loss of loved ones, you name it. I'd lose my mind over hearing the word man over and over. The thought of someone losing their mind over a word is childish; therefore, I must be a child, and if that's the case, maybe I *can* sell candy to kids.

    The Women's Circle and the Voyeurs are about tied in the war. The Old Men are definitely losing. Bob Billings's death has never been and will never be avenged. No one else has died, but bones have been broken, bodies bruised, and one of the women was set on fire this past Tuesday. Her flaming body ran past me while I stocked some Fun Time Cookies. Gary, Raven, and Stan keep pressuring me to join a side. I tell them I need more time; they tell me my time is running out. Nothing too bad has happened to me yet. I did get hit in the back of the head with a can of Handout Tuna. The Old Men tell me the Women did it. The Women tell me it was the Voyeurs. The Voyeurs tell me something else. I can't trust anyone at Rudy's. I should be able to trust Henry, but he's become one of my greatest enemies. I think he pretended to be my best friend all these years so he could collect all my secrets and use them against me. It's not good when people know too much about you. The more someone knows, the more powerful they become. At Rudy's, we're forced to wear these stupid name tags. This weakens employees and strengthens customers. Whenever someone says my name, I shrink up inside. I don't want customers knowing my name. Imagine what would happen if I lost this name tag and some crazy person found it. I can hear the police radios now: "ALL UNITS! ALL UNITS! Be on the lookout for a man wearing a Rudy's Grocery name tag with the name TOM! *T* as in *terrified*, *o* as in *of*, and *m* as in *mango*. *Tom!* This man is extremely dangerous! Shoot to kill!" Now I can't even go outside anymore. I have to grow a beard, dye my hair, and live in the woods for the rest of my life. Thanks, Rudy's!

"Where is your soup located?" asks customer.

"In the soup aisle," I say.

"Thought so," responds customer. "Just wanted to double-check."

"Why are the back-of-the-box cooking directions always a minute or so off?" asks another customer.

"I'm not sure," I say.

"I'll tell you why. The people conducting the microwave tests are all slackers. You think they're actually microwaving the products? No way! They're just taking guesses."

"My sister's angry at my mom, who's angry at my dad, who's angry at me for talking to my mom, which angered my sister, which angered my mom, which angered my dad and led to me not talking to my mom, my dad, or my sister," explains yet another customer. "Are you following me?"

There are signs posted throughout Rudy's that read *The customer is always right.* No one is *always* right. I hope whoever created that phrase is dead and spending his or her eternity surrounded by customers. *Where's this? Where's that? Where's the manager? These prices are too high. It's cold in here. It's hot in here. What's this taste like? What's that taste like? What does it take to get some decent service around here?! I want a refund! I'm never shopping here again! When do you close? When do you open? When will you stop fighting us?*

Dear Mr. Jim,

Your Life Improvement Kit does not work. I did the exercises, wore the T-shirt, and tried my hardest to <u>not</u> think. Anyway, please refund my money. I am having some roommate troubles and could use the extra cash to pay the bills.

Tom Mitchell

I am reaching the point where I don't care anymore. That's what I think, at least, but what I think and what I do are two separate things. I don't know if I'll ever actually do anything. I can think all I want, but what's the point of all this thinking? Has it gotten me anywhere? If anything, it's messed me up. Held me back. I am nothing on the outside because I keep everything on the inside.

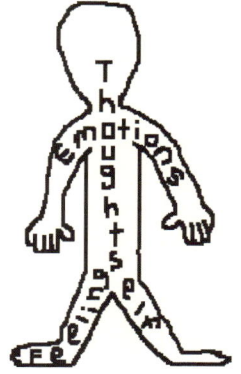

Gary catches me spying on Henry and the High School and College Kids and compliments me on my "natural talent." I get the whole idea about people pursuing what they're good at, but I don't want to be known as a guy who's good at watching people. I'm not sure what I want to be known for. That's the only reason people live: to be known. If all I do with my life is work at Rudy's, I'm pretty much nothing. I don't even want people *seeing* me work here, let alone *knowing* me for it. At least if I were known for watching people, I'd have that, and I think being known as a people-watcher would be better than being known for a nothing Rudy's Grocery store employee. But then again, being known as a guy who watches people makes me sound like some sort of weirdo. I don't even like people who watch birds.

Recurring Nightmare:

There are unsatisfied customers coming at me from both ends of the bread aisle. I stand in the middle as they move in closer and closer. They've found out what I really think of them. They're not happy. They corner me and tear me limb from limb. My body parts are scattered throughout Rudy's. My legs are in the cereal aisle. My arms are in the ice cream freezer. My torso is in the condiment aisle. And my head is sitting with the watermelons.

I'm learning to live on my own. No friends, no groups, no nothing. People think they need other people, but it's not true. I fooled myself into thinking I needed Henry. I don't need him. I'm perfectly fine on my own. A lot of people have backup friends they hang out with if the main friend is not working out, but having a whole bunch of friends was never my style. I would rather have one friend who I can talk to and hang out with than juggle a handful of friend-ships. It's too much work. Say instead of Henry, I ran with three main friends: Tim, Julie, and Joe. Tim and I are friends because we like movies, Julie and I are friends because we read magazines, and Joe and I are friends because we make each other laugh. It's a lot easier to be friends with one person who likes movies, reads magazines, and makes me laugh than to deal with three separate people. I don't want to have to keep track of everything that's going on in all these people's lives. There are birthdays, get-togethers, and all sorts of stuff going on. I can't deal with that. And there can be so many complications. What if I feel like reading magazines but Julie's not around? Then I have to hang out with Joe and Tim and fake-laugh and pretend to be interested in movies. And that's just three friends! What happens if I go to some off-the-wall party with Tim, Julie, and Joe, and everyone's approaching me and saying, "Hey, you look cool. Let's hang out." I make a little chitchat and leave the party not only friends with Tim, Julie, and Joe, but also friends with Russ, Sam, Maria, Amy, Kate, Bill, and Keith. And all these people have something different in common with me. Russ likes a band I like, Sam and I like fast food, Maria's into aliens, Amy's got a cool car, Kate works at an arcade, Bill can get discounts on massages, and Keith's got a dog. Now I'm juggling all sorts of information. I have to create detailed charts just to keep track of everyone. "Okay, Amy's got the cool car, Maria likes talking aliens, Sam does . . . what the hell does Sam do?" I'll eventually gather so many friends that I'll forget their names and why I'm even friends with them. Next thing I know, I'm at Bill's place talking aliens when he doesn't even like aliens. He likes massages! Word gets out that I'm a bad friend, and eventually everyone ends up hating me.

Are you an annoying customer? Do employees secretly hate you? Find out by reading the list below:

Annoying Customer List

1. Walk into a store and immediately ask for help.
2. Ask employee to "check the back" after they already tell you that the item is out of stock.

3. Spend more than ten minutes in an aisle.
4. Ask employee for directions to a good restaurant.
5. Ask employee more than three questions in a row.
6. Talk about the old Rudy's and how much better it was.
7. Expect employee to know *everything* about *every* single product.
8. Give shopping carts to (or take them from) employee in the parking lot.
9. Ask employee, "Can I get this cheaper somewhere else?"
10. Make stupid comments about out-of-stock items. "This whole store is out of stock!"
11. Comment on employee's uniform.
12. Comment on prices being too high.
13. Ask employee for store coupons.
14. Ask employee for help carrying your bags when you are perfectly capable of doing it yourself.
15. Ask employee to call another grocery store for any reason.
16. Breathe loudly.
17. Ask employee to get the manager.
18. Call employee by their name.
19. Complain to employee about the store's layout.
20. Wear a shirt tied around your neck.
21. Leave garbage in shopping carts.
22. Talk to employee about your personal life.
23. Accuse employee of shorting you money.
24. Ask for paper bags.
25. Ask for double paper bags.
26. Put items back in the wrong location.
27. Talk too close to employee's face.
28. Touch employee.

29. Talk back to employee.
30. Make employee throw out your garbage.

I've stopped eating at Night Burger. I am having Space Sticks withdrawal. I don't feel like myself. I've been thinking about killing customers. Don't worry; my stupid No-Bother Policy restricts me from harming others. Plus, customer killing is too much of a hassle. I'd have to go out and buy gloves, knives, garbage bags, and rope, and then I'd have to dispose of the body. Maybe if I got paid to kill customers, it would be a different story, but most successful businesses need their customers alive.

I'm falling deeper and deeper into this headspace or whatever you call it. I'm losing my grip on reality. I live in a pretend world. I make up things. I fool myself into thinking that what I'm saying is real. People fool themselves all the time. I'm holding onto things I shouldn't. Thoughts enter my mind by the thousands. I can't keep them straight. They all tell me different things. I've reached that point where I have to figure out who I am or something. Grow up. Be a man. *Man . . . man . . . man.* I'm starting to lose it. I can feel it. I'm not living a normal life. I don't even know what a normal life is. I know that a normal life isn't happiness. I see bad in everything. The only good thing I got going for me is my toilet paper collection. I like opening the trunk and staring at all the rolls. It makes me feel proud.

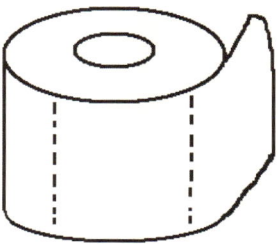

"TOM MITCHELL OUT FOR CARTS. TOM MITCHELL OUT FOR CARTS."

I stock the last few packages of Time's Up Tamales and head to the break room to grab my sweatshirt and steal a toilet paper roll. I never thought I'd become a toilet paper thief, but when you're living in a state of nothing, you sometimes become something you don't expect.

I push open the break room door. There are three old men standing inside.

"It's time," says the one wearing khaki shorts and calf socks.

"Time for what?" I ask.

"Your final warning."

We stand in silence.

The other two old men look like twins. Their faces droop down the same.

"I have to use the bathroom," I say.

I try to leave, but the door's locked.

"Warm out today," one of the twins says.

"Huh?"

"Seventy-four degrees," responds the other twin.

"Not a cloud in the sky," says the old man with the shorts and socks.

I feel dizzy.

"Wind from the southwest at approximately ten miles per hour."

"Only thirty percent humidity."

I stumble to the break table and sit down. I fight to stay awake. "What are you doing to me?" I ask.

"They're talking upper seventies all week."

"Great golfing weather."

"Superb golfing weather."

"Outstanding golfing weather."

My eyes close and I fall asleep.

fourteen

BOB WALKED to the back of the tiny office and opened a big cardboard box.

"What size shirt are you?" he asked.

"Medium."

I sat in one of the metal folding chairs while he dug around inside. The Night Burger office was nothing like the dining room. There were no wall paintings, no star ceiling, no random sound effects. It was just a small room with white walls, a desk, two metal folding chairs, and three gray filing cabinets. On the office door hung a framed picture of some guy with long white hair and sunglasses.

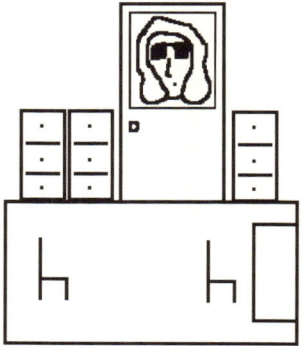

"Here." Bob pulled a shirt from the cardboard box and threw it at me. It was the famous blue collared shirt with miniature Night Burger moon logo stitched on the chest.

"Wow," I said.

"Yeah, impressive," Bob replied. "How tall are you?"

"About five foot seven."

Bob resumed searching inside the box. I couldn't believe I was holding an actual Night Burger shirt.

"These should fit."

Something hit me in the face and fell to the floor. The pants. I picked them up. They were the classic black pants with thin blue stripe running down both sides. I stood and held them against my legs.

"Enough of that." Bob walked toward me and plopped the legendary green hat (also with Night Burger moon logo) on top of my head. "You'll get your name tag tomorrow."

He grabbed a clipboard off his desk.

"I have you starting at eleven. Be here fifteen minutes early so we can go over some training stuff."

"Okay."

Bob tossed the clipboard back on the desk and lit a cigarette. "You can grab a plastic bag from up front to toss all
that shit in."

I flew home on my bike and headed straight to my bedroom. I closed the door and laid the uniform out on my bed.
It looked like a superhero costume. I wasn't going to be the
same Tom Mitchell anymore. I now had a job to do. I took
off my clothes and put on the uniform, tucking the blue shirt
into the black pants and adjusting the green hat to fit my
head. Once everything was on, I walked over to my dresser
mirror.

"Whoa." Everything looked perfect. "Greetings, earthlings! Welcome to Night Burger! Would you like to try our
famous Burger Classic meal?"

I was a natural. The words came out like I'd been saying
them my whole life. I fell backward onto my bed and stared
at the ceiling. I was only fifteen years old and an official
Night Burger employee. Soon I would discover some of the
greatest mysteries and secrets ever. Everything I wanted to
know about Night Burger would finally be revealed: how
the food was made, who drew the wall paintings, and who,
or what life form, actually owned the place.

"Check it out," I said as I unzipped my jacket.

"Holy crap!" Henry jumped off his bed. "You got the
job!"

I had a big smile on my face. "Yep."

"That's awesome!"

I tossed my jacket on the carpet. "I have the pants and hat back home."

"You should have brought them over."

"I was going to, but I need to keep them safe."

Henry walked around me in a circle.

"I look good, right?"

"Yeah," Henry said.

"Feel this fabric."

He touched my right sleeve. "It's soft."

"Softest fabric on Earth," I replied. "It's probably from some crazy alien planet."

Slight pause. "So when do you start?"

"Tomorrow," I said. "I have to be there at ten forty-five."

"You're working the afternoon shift*?"

"Yeah. I'm not too happy about it."

Henry sat on his bed and started flipping through TV channels. I grabbed a pillow from his closet and sat on the floor.

"You should apply," I said.

"I have weight training."

"All summer?"

"Yep."

"You can always quit football."

"I can't," Henry replied. "The team needs me."

---

* Night Burger looked like a completely different restaurant during the afternoon. The big white moon wasn't lit up, and the orange, yellow, and blue outdoor lights were all turned off. The inside was different too. Sunlight spilled in through the round windows. The black star ceiling was off, tables didn't glow, wall paintings looked dull, and the speakers blared news radio.

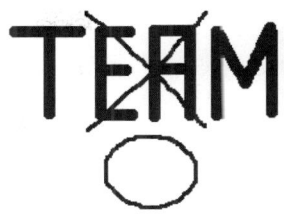

I told my parents the good news during dinner.

"Never heard of it," said my mom.

"It's down Davis Street."

"By Smith's Park?" asked my dad. "Pass the potatoes."

"Farther up the street," I said. "After the woods on the left."

"What's it called again?" my mom asked. "You want more meat?"

"No, thanks," answered my dad.

"Night Burger."

"Sounds cheap," remarked my mom.

"The food's really good," I said. "Can I have more vegetables?"

"How are you getting there?" asked my dad.

"Thanks." I scooped some green beans onto my plate. "I'm going to ride my bike."

"Those cars drive fast on Davis Street."

"I know."

"And you start tomorrow?" my mom asked.

I chewed and swallowed. "Yeah."

"What time?"

"I have to be there at ten forty-five."

"Perfect," said my mom. "My shows start at eleven."

The next morning I woke up early, ate breakfast, showered, got dressed, and left around nine. I took my time biking to Night Burger and made sure everyone saw me by riding slowly in the middle of the road. A bunch of cars honked at me. Some drivers even yelled out their windows. The beeps and shouts made me feel like a real-life super-hero. I created a theme song in my head and made Henry my sidekick. His costume wasn't as cool as mine, but he did whatever I wanted and protected me from enemies. He also didn't have any other friends. It was just me and him, and together, we were saving the world.

Superheroes

A dirty old beat-up car pulled into the Night Burger parking lot. It was Bob. He had his window rolled down and a cigarette hanging from his lips. He parked and stumbled out of his car. His hair was all messy like he'd just woken up.

"You been waiting long?" he asked as he walked over.

"No," I said.

He tossed his cigarette on the pavement and unlocked the revolving door. "That your bike?"

"Yes."

"I used to ride my bike up here." Bob stood there a moment. "Come on."

We pushed through the revolving door and made our way inside. All the lights were turned off and everything was quiet. I stood and watched as Bob relocked the front door and walked back by the cash registers. "Check this out."

I followed him behind the main counter. He was kneeling and pointing to this control panel of different-colored switches.

"These are the switches," he explained. "They turn on the lights and shit. The three red cnes control the kitchen lighting." He flipped the switches. The whole kitchen area lit up. "These stay on all day and night."

I nodded.

"These four green switches are for the day shift." He flipped them all up and the dining room came to life. "We run these from open till five. The six blue switches here are for night. We run those from five till close. Blue switches, night. Green switches, day. Red switches, day and night."

Bob stood up.

"The music switch is outside my office. Don't ask me why."

We walked through the kitchen.

"Here." He pointed to two switches. One marked Sound FX and the other News Radio. "We play news radio open till five and the sound effects after."

He flicked the News Radio switch.

"A man was killed today after falling off a ladder. Sources say the man lost his balance and broke his neck on the ground below . . ."

"Why is the day setup so different from night?" I asked.

"Our daytime customers are mainly adults who don't like all that darkness and cheesy space shit."

Bob entered the office and grabbed something off his desk. "Here's your name tag."

"Thanks."

Bob nodded and lit a cigarette.

I undid the back pin and carefully attached the green tag to my blue shirt.

"You familiar with the Night Burger language?" Bob asked.

"Kind of."

He opened one of the filing cabinet drawers and took out a sheet of paper. "This sheet tells you what everything means."

I couldn't believe I was getting this sort of confidential information on my first day. I grabbed the sheet from him. "Can I keep this?"

"Yeah."

I looked it over. There were a bunch of phrases I'd never heard before: *Warp Speed. May I see your Earth Identification Card? Sorry about the wait, but there was a recent alien invasion.*

"You don't have to memorize all that shit. They want us to, but fuck it." Bob tossed his cigarette into an old drink cup. "Any questions?"

"No."

"Good."

We left the office and entered the kitchen area. Bob gave me a quick tour and showed me the grill, fryer, cash registers, freezer, sink, cleaning supplies, storage bins, and where to hang our coats.

"You didn't bring a coat today, right?" Bob asked.

"No."

"Well, if you do, make sure to hang it up back here," he said. "It will start smelling like shit if you leave it anywhere else."

Bob walked toward a gray metal door marked EXIT. "The Dumpster's out back." He pushed open the door and pointed. "There. Also, this door locks from the inside, so whenever you use it, prop it open with that small piece of wood on the floor there next to the sink."

I looked by the sink and saw the small piece of wood. Bob closed the door.

"You smoke?" he asked.

"No."

"Well, if you start, you can smoke out this back door. I'm the only one allowed to smoke inside."

KNOCK! KNOCK! KNOCK!

"Shit," Bob said.

We hurried up front to the dining room. Someone was standing outside the revolving door.

"Is that a customer?" I asked.

"No," Bob said as he unlocked the door. "Employee."

The revolving door started moving and some guy walked inside. He looked to be in his mid-thirties and wore a gray sweatshirt and the same black pants with blue stripes as me.

"Tom, this is Bruce. Bruce, Tom."

"Hey," Bruce said as he plopped his green Night Burger hat on his head.

"Hello," I replied.

Bruce unzipped his sweatshirt and walked into the back.

"Bruce works the grill," Bob said. "He'll show you some stuff later."

More employees started showing up. I met them all as they came in.

"Hello," I said to each one. "I'm Tom."

My first week was devoted to training. I rotated through all the different stations and learned how everything worked. Bruce taught me the grill. Andrea taught me the cash registers. Dave taught me the drive-thru. Bonnie taught me how to clean the dining room. Jeff taught me the Fueling Station. Tina taught me dishes. Leo taught me bathrooms. And Shawn taught me the fryer.

Out of everyone I trained with, the only employee who talked about the *secrets* was Shawn.

"This restaurant isn't normal," he told me during my orientation to Space Sticks and Orbit Rings. "There's a lot of extraterrestrial stuff going on."

"I believe you, Shawn," I said.

"You do?!"

"Sure. Ever since my first visit to Night Burger with my friend Henry, I knew something was up."

"You have friends?" asked Shawn.

"Just one."

He scratched his oily face and told me how it was important to keep this alien stuff secret because talking about "the unexplained" makes people look at you funny. Apparently all the other employees thought Shawn was crazy.

"I'm not crazy," he told me as he lifted the fryer baskets out of the boiling grease. "Listen to this. So the food is always delivered late at night, okay?"

"Uh-huh."

"So I'm thinking, what's up with that, right? So I do an all-night stakeout in the woods across the street. Guess what? Around 3 a.m., the delivery truck pulls up. Let me tell you, there's a reason why the food is shipped overnight."

"Why's that?" I asked.

"The guys delivering it are green and have six eyes and six legs."

One of the many perks of working at Night Burger was the free pop. Employees could drink as much as they wanted. My favorite was Saturn Fizz, a strawberry-flavored fizzy drink. My second favorite was Cosmic X, third was Orbit Blast, fourth was a tie between, Solar Bliss, Blue Meteor, Fifth Dimension, and Star Bubble, and my least favorite was The Missing Link. Sometimes I mixed all the pops together. I called that drink The Universe because it contained all the different flavors. Sometimes it tasted good and other times tasted bad. One time, I mixed the pops and made the best-tasting Universe ever. I tried duplicating the process but could never quite figure it out.

Henry and I hung out and watched TV whenever we could. I talked a lot about Night Burger. I left out the boring parts like taking out the trash and scrubbing the toilets and sweating over the hot fryer. Sometimes I made things up about Night Burger to make the job sound cooler than it actually was.

"We just got this robot that cooks and does all the work," I told him once. "All we do is sit around and eat free food."

The weekly work schedule was posted every Tuesday outside Bob's office. I was assigned the afternoon shift all summer, but when school started up, I switched to nights. The latest I ever worked was 9 p.m. Bob never scheduled me to close, which, according to Shawn, was "prime alien time." One night, I got stuck washing the dishes till almost 10 p.m. and heard these strange noises in my ear. It wasn't the random sound effects or anything like that. It was like I was picking up some sort of secret talk. I told Shawn about it and he said he knew all about hearing voices.

"What does it mean?" I asked.

"They're trying to communicate with you."

None of the employees seemed to like one another. Pretty much everyone talked behind each other's backs. It reminded me of high school. Some employees actually went to my high school. I recognized their faces. Since I wasn't friends with any of them, I acted like I'd never seen them before. They did the same.

Bob hid out in his office the majority of the time and smoked cigarettes. He told me smoking was the only thing in life that he enjoyed anymore. Supposedly he'd been working at Night Burger since it opened. I don't ever remember seeing him. He said he looks a lot different now.

"This place destroys everyone differently," he explained. "Sure, it aged me about ten years, but at least I didn't end up like Dennis."

"Who's Dennis?" I asked.

"The old manager."

"What happened to him?"

"He blew his brains out."

A few months into the job, I was taken off fryer and general cleaning duty and promoted to drive-thru. I loved wearing the black headset and pretending I was a space commander.

"Base, come in. This is Commander Tom."

"This is Base."

"The Burger Prince has once again taken control of the Burger Galaxy. Send reinforcements. Repeat: send reinforcements."

"What is your current location, Commander?"

"I'm currently on planet Zoot, outside the Ding Lounge."

"Get to the High Rocks and we'll have the mother ship pick you up."

"I can't," I said. "The Burger Prince has taken my friend Kalmax and his brother's rock band hostage. I must rescue them."

"There's no time—"

Beep. Beep. Beep.

I grabbed my order book and pen and activated my headset. The beeping stopped.

"Greetings, earthlings!"

"One minute," a voice replied.

"Sure," I said. "Let me know when you're ready for liftoff."

My communications with Base were constantly interrupted by hungry earthlings.

"Hello?" the voice eventually said. "Hello!"

"Yes, earthling, how can I help you?"

"I want three Night Burgers, two orders of Orbit Rings, a medium Missing Link with no ice, a medium Saturn Fizz, and a medium Orbit Blast."

I wrote everything down on my order pad and repeated the order as I rang it up on the cash register. "I got three Night Burgers, two orders of Orbit Rings, medium Missing Link no ice, medium Saturn Fizz, and medium Orbit Blast. Would you like to try our Unidentified Apple Crumble for dessert?"

"No, thanks."

"Your total is thirteen sixty-six. Please pull your spacecraft around to the eye of the universe."

I ripped the top page off my order pad and stuck it on the order wheel for Bruce and Shawn to read. I walked back to the round drive-thru window and pushed it open.

"Thirteen sixty-six, please."

Inside the car was an old man and two young kids in the back seat who were bouncing around and laughing loudly. I always loved going through the drive-thru when I was a kid. I thought it was pretty amazing how we didn't even have to get out of the car to get the food.

The old man opened his wallet and handed me a twenty.

"Thanks," I said. "I'll be right back with your change and Mission Report."

I closed the drive-thru window and cashed out the order.

"Six thirty-four is your change. Here's your Mission Report. Your rocket fuel will be right up."

I quickly filled each pop and applied the clear plastic lid. I always liked pushing down the bubble tabs that told the customers what kind of pop it was. Once the tabs were pushed, I grabbed one of the cardboard drink carriers and inserted the pops. I tossed in three straws and stuffed some napkins in the one empty slot.

"Here is your rocket fuel," I said as I handed the old man the drink carrier. "Your food will be landing shortly."

I loved saying that last line. "Your food will be landing shortly." It made me feel like I was in charge. I leaned against the drive-thru ledge and watched Bruce and Shawn work. I often thought of the whole order-taking and drink-getting process as a race between me and the cooks, and I loved winning.

While leaning against the drive-thru ledge, I heard a knock. I ignored it at first, thinking it came from inside the store. Seconds later, I heard it again. Someone was knocking on the drive-thru window. I turned around and pushed it open.

"This isn't right," the old man said as he handed me back the drinks. "I wanted no ice. I specifically said no ice."

The two kids in the backseat were still and quiet.

"I didn't put ice in the Missing Link," I replied.

"I said no ice each drink."

I set the drink carrier on the ledge and grabbed my order book: medium Missing Link no ice, medium Saturn Fizz, and medium Orbit Blast.

"My ticket says no ice for the Missing Link and that's all," I said.

"I said no ice for all three."

"Are you sure?" I asked.

"Are you stupid?! I said *NO* goddamn ice! *ALL* drinks! Now fix it!"

I closed the drive-thru window and emptied the Saturn Fizz and Orbit Blast into the sink. I could have sworn he said no ice for only the Missing Link. *Did he say no ice for all the drinks? He must have. I messed up. It's my fault.* I hurried to refill the pops.

"Drive-thru! Three Night Burgers, two Orbit Rings!" Bruce yelled.

The food was ready. I had lost the race.

There were more angry customers. Many more. Some yelled about their food being cold. Others complained about the quality of our napkins. Many accused me of shorting them change. Not giving them enough ketchup. The Space Sticks were too salty. The parking lot was too small. The outside moon was too bright. *Turn down those crappy sound effects!* The pop was flat. The food overpriced. Jerk. Loser. *Asshole!* I tried to ignore it all but couldn't.

"I don't know if I can work the drive-thru anymore," I told Bob one night.

"Why's that?" he asked.

"The customers," I said. "I don't understand why they're so angry."

"That's just how customers are," he said as he lit a cigarette. "You'll eventually get used to it."

fifteen

A BRIGHT BEAM OF LIGHT shines on my shirt. Then another on my pants. Then another on my face. Then another and another until my entire body is covered in light. I feel like I'm about to be abducted by aliens and brought onto the mother ship. I lift my arms high into the air to embrace the moment.

"Put your arms down," a voice commands.

I do as I'm told and stare at my shoes to avoid the bright lights.

"Mr. Tom Mitchell," says the voice.

"Yes," I reply.

"My name is Walter, and I am the leader of the Old Men, protector of the back room and keeper of your darkest secrets. I have summoned you here today to make you one final membership offer."

Grumbling starts from every direction. I never knew if Walter really existed, but I guess he does. His voice is very deep. It's probably like that from talking all the time. Leaders have to talk. I've never heard of a non-talking leader.

"SILENCE!" The grumbling stops.

"To begin," Walter's deep voice says, "I'd like to ask Mr. Mitchell a question. Mr. Mitchell, why have you refused to join us?"

I don't know what to say. I shouldn't even be involved in this stupid war. "I'd really like to stay out of the war if possible."

The grumbling starts up again.

"SILENCE!"

I continue staring at my shoes.

"Listen carefully, Mr. Mitchell. You are part of this war whether you like it or not."

"Why?" I ask.

"You must decide where you belong. This childlike indecision of yours has gone on long enough."

"I—"

"Before you speak," Walter interrupts, "let me remind you that we can protect you from both the Women's Circle and the Voyeurs. Our members are loyal fighters who will die to protect their own. Yes, we are old, but together, we are wise. You are very important to us, Mr. Mitchell. Your internal anger toward customers is much more powerful than you think. If channeled correctly, we can use that anger to destroy our enemies and *win the war!*"

Raspy cheering.

"Join us and there will be no more customers! You will be protected by the walls of the back room and free from all those . . . *questions.*"

More raspy cheering.

"SILENCE!"

The cheering stops.

"However, if you betray us and join the Women's Circle or the Voyeurs, we will have no choice but to inform the world of your angry customer thoughts. This will cause you severe anguish for the remainder of your natural life. No more golf, bingo, shuffleboard. NO MORE WALKS! Everything you know and love will be taken from you as you will become the most hated thirty-six-year-old man alive."

"I'm actually twenty-six."

"SILENCE! You have one final week to decide."

The lights slowly disappear from my body until only one remains on my chest.

"Take three steps forward."

I do as I'm told.

The one remaining light disappears and the back room turns black. Two old men grab me by the arms while another wraps a blindfold over my eyes.

"You will be visited by the other two groups today. They will offer you similar protection and deliver similar threats. Know that our protection is the best and our threats are the most severe. Stan will provide you with a benefits brochure on your way out. Join us, Tom! Join us in the back room and help us win the war! *Join us!*"

The entire back room starts chanting: "Join us! Join us! Join us!"

I'm nudged in the back and blindly led into the darkness. A few moments later, the two Old Men guiding me sit me down in a chair and tell me to count to sixty.

"One, two, three . . ."

When I finish counting, I remove the blindfold. It takes my eyes a minute or so to adjust. I'm sitting alone at the break room table. Not as cool as being on an alien mother ship. Directly in front of me is a tan brochure with a cover that reads: *The Benefits of Becoming an Old Man.*

"Mitchell!" Pete yells. "Where the heck ya been?"

"I was in the bathroom."

"For a half-hour?"

"My stomach's been messed up."

"You better not have used up all that toilet paper."

Henry and the High School and College Kids walk past. They point and laugh.

"Arms up," Pete says. "Let me check those pockets."

I lift my arms. Pete pats me down.

"At ease, Mitchell."

I lower my arms.

"Listen," Pete says. "I need that A-Plus ketchup endcap swapped out with Villayne's Peanut Butter pronto."

"What about carts?" I ask.

"What carts?"

"Didn't someone call me out for carts?"

"Are you taking dope, Mitchell?"

"No."

Pete gets right up in my face. Sweat drips down his bald head. He's trying to get me to crack. "Get to work."

"Excuse me, sir," says some woman in a yellow raincoat. "Is the A-Plus Ketchup still on sale?"

"No, sorry," I say as I pull the remaining ketchup bottles from the endcap and set them inside my empty shopping cart. "The sale ended yesterday."

"Can I still get the sale price?"

"I don't think so."

"But it's only been one day."

"I know, but—"

"I'd like to speak with the manager."

I used to think that all customers were oblivious brain-dead idiots, but that's not the case. They know exactly what they're doing. Like, right now, this woman knows she's being a pain in the ass. Life is all about power and control. *Give me the sale price! Get the manager!* She demands things from me because it makes her feel important. I'm sure that in her real life, like most people, she has nothing. No power. No control. No anything. But once she steps foot inside Rudy's, she transforms into a customer—a person who has power and control and everything they could ever want.

"Like I was telling Tom," the woman explains to Pete, "it's only been one day."

"I understand," Pete says. "We'll take care of it."

The woman smiles as she removes two ketchup bottles from my cart and places them in hers. I smile back and imagine her drowning in her yellow raincoat. It's not even raining outside. She dresses for weather that doesn't exist. That says a lot about her personality. You can tell all sorts of things about people by the way they dress. Sweatpants people are lazy. Suit people think they're super important. If you see someone wearing a cowboy hat, RUN. Trust me.

While waiting for my Villayne's Peanut Butter stock, I browse through my *Benefits of Becoming an Old Man* brochure. I'm not too crazy about the Personality Profiles section. Every Old Man's main interest is talking about the weather. I do, however, love the Back Room Getaway section. One hundred percent security. Back lot parking. No customers, non-members, or managers allowed. They also have bathrooms, putting greens, electronic massage chairs, and even a hot tub back there.

The back room door opens. My peanut butter stock is rolled out on a six-wheeler by the tall, muscular, stone-faced door guard.

"Thanks," I say.

The giant cracks his knuckles and closes the door.

Customers walk past and comment while I stock the peanut butter endcap.

"It's about time your peanut butter went on sale."

"Is your jelly on sale too?"

"Villayne's! Yuck!"

I have yet to see Gary or Raven. The Old Men told me I was going to be visited by all three groups. I hope they've forgotten about me. Most people don't want to be forgotten. I am the complete opposite. I want to be forgotten. The more people forget me, the more freedom I have. I don't want to be in anyone's mind, thoughts, or anything. I don't want to exist.

The office door opens.

"Can I go on my lunch break?" I ask Pete.

"That endcap done?"

"Yes."

"Go. And no funny business."

Just as I'm about to grab a box of Magic O's off the shelf, my *Benefits of Becoming an Old Man* brochure is yanked from my back pocket. I turn around. Gary.

"This looks attractive," he says as he flips through the pages. "Ooh, hot tub."

"Can I have that back?"

Gary pulls a tiny silver bell out of his tight red pants pocket and gives it a ring. Steve a.k.a. Peek and Cory the Cork come crawling out of the shelves. Cereal boxes fall to the floor. Peek and Cory dust themselves off and stand next to Gary.

"I should be going," I say as I grab the Magic O's.

Gary smiles and points to the cereal box. "Date with Lisa?"

"I don't do that anymore."

"You don't have to lie to us, Tom."

"Can I have my brochure back?"

Gary smiles and sticks the brochure down his tight red pants.

"I need that."

Gary, Peek, and Cory snicker. I turn to leave.

"Freeze, Tom," Gary says.

I stop.

"Turn around."

I do what he says.

"Take five steps toward me."

One. Two. Three. Four. Five.

"Good boy," Gary replies. "You're not joining the Old Men."

"I didn't say I was."

"Ooh!" Gary looks wide-eyed at Peek and Cory. "I like when he takes control."

Cory's butt plug starts buzzing. I step back. Gary shoots him an angry look. "Not now!" Cory nods and reaches into his pocket. "Sorry, boss." The buzzing stops.

"Let's cut to the chase, Tom. You have one week to choose a side. Now, I don't know what those Old Men told you, but know this: whatever they said is a lie." Gary runs his fingers across his thin mustache. "You really think they have a hot tub back there?"

"I don't know."

"Look, Tom. We are winning the war, and once we do, we will have access to the entire store. Including the back room. You can be King of the Back Room if you want. You have my word." Gary pauses. "Have the women contacted you yet?"

I don't say anything.

"Doesn't matter," Gary says. "You even think about going against us, and every employee will find out what you really are—an Employee Voyeur. The employees will want you dead, and your chances of ever being with little Lisa will go bye-bye forever."

Gary, Peek, and Cory smile.

"This is what you are, Tom. You're not a woman or an old man. You're a voyeur. You watch people. It's in your blood. Stop denying the truth and join us!"

Gary touches my hand. I pull back.

"Wow," he says. "Great reflexes."

"I have to go." I turn and walk down the aisle.

"Sure thing," he yells. "You have one week."

I look back and see Peek and Cory crawling back into the shelves. Gary picks up the fallen cereal boxes off the floor and puts them back into place. Before I turn the corner, all three voyeurs are gone.

"Nine thirty-three," says Carol.

I open my wallet and hand her a ten-dollar bill.

"Thanks," she says.

I only bought a box of Magic O's and a quart of milk. I should have had Lisa ring me up. The cereal and milk would have been great conversation starter.

"Yeah, I eat pretty healthy."

"I can see that," Lisa would say.

"Maybe you can come over sometime and we can eat cereal together."

"I'd like that."

"Your change," Carol says as she drops the coins on the counter.

"Thank you," I say as I scoop them up. "Can I have a receipt?"

"No."

I unlock my car door and get in. The interior smells like hair spray.

"Hello, Tom."

I turn around and find Raven lying in my back seat.

"What's going on?" I ask.

"Face forward, eat your cereal, and act normal."

I do what she says. She might have a gun. Whenever a stranger appears in the back seat of your car, they typically have a gun.

"I know you were visited by the Old Men and the Voyeurs."

I open the cereal box and eat some Magic O's.

"Have you made your decision?" she asks.

"No. I supposedly have one more week to decide."

"Hear this, Tom. We are living in powerful and dangerous times. Times where anything is possible and good can rise above evil. You must trust me when I say that you need to join the Women's Circle."

"But I'm not a woman."

"Don't worry," she says. "The women have agreed to accept you."

"I don't understand why I have to join one of these groups."

"That's life. You can't go on living in this world by yourself."

"Why not?"

"Because living alone will destroy you."

I open the milk and take a sip.

"You need us," Raven continues. "Our army is stronger and more powerful than the Old Men and the Voyeurs combined. We offer support, guidance, and protection. No other group offers that. We also know your real age."

"I do like that," I say.

"You'll like it all," Raven replies. "I know it."

"What happens if I join one of the other two groups instead?"

"You will become our enemy, and the women will spread vicious rumors that will ruin your life and destroy your friendship with Henry forever."

"Our friendship's already destroyed."

"Not exactly," says Raven.

"How do you even know about Henry?" I ask.

"We've known about him for a while. We have a very detailed file on you, Tom."

"And why can I trust you?"

"I wish I could tell you, but I can't. It would jeopardize both our lives as well as my position as leader of the Women's Circle."

"I still don't understand why I'm being dragged into this."

"You are a threat to us and everyone else at Rudy's."

"I'm only one person, though."

"You have one week," she says. "I hope you make the right decision."

Raven opens the back door and flies out.

sixteen

ABOUT A WEEK after graduating high school, I received a letter in the mail. It came in a plain white envelope with no return address. I didn't open it right away. I don't trust letters with no return address. There was this TV show Henry and I used to watch called *Quantum*. It was about two salesmen: Sam, who was really tall, and Troy, who was really short. Anyway, Sam and Troy were the best salesmen at Quantum Technologies. They could sell anything to anyone. In fact, they were so good that their boss, Zeek Peppers, decided to team them up. Neither Sam nor Troy was happy about the partnership. Since Sam was tall, he didn't understand anything about Troy, and since Troy was short, he didn't understand anything about Sam. They only thing they understood about one another was the job of being a salesman.

In one episode, Sam received a letter with no return address. Troy warned him against opening it. Since Sam didn't trust Troy, he opened it anyway. The letter ended up being from this Stanley guy who was mad at Sam for selling him some faulty merchandise. Stanley wrote how the transaction ruined his marriage. *Thanks to you and your crappy stereo equipment, my wife left me for a less gullible man.* Alone with a crappy stereo and no wife, Stanley became depressed and suicidal. He started cutting on himself and spent eight months in the local psych ward. When he got out, he was determined to do one thing and one thing only—kill Sam.

If Sam would have put his tallness aside and listened to Troy, he would have never opened the letter and therefore know nothing about Stanley. Instead, Sam will now live the rest of his life knowing that there's some insane murderous unsatisfied customer after him. It was summer vacation and I wasn't about to deal with any of that, so I hid my no-return-address letter inside my dresser drawer.

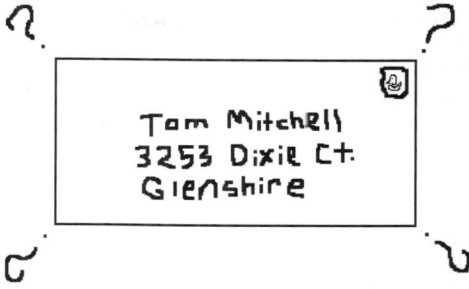

I planned to work at Night Burger all summer but quit shortly after high school graduation. When I first started, the job was magical, but as the years passed, I began to hate it. I was tired of cooking, cleaning, working the drive-thru, running the cash register, seeing the employees (besides Shawn, who was either abducted by aliens or killed by one of the employees), and most importantly, I was tired of dealing with the customers. They drove me insane with their demands and negative attitudes. Bob told me that I'd get used to it, but I never did. I took in all the insults and complaints and locked them away inside my mind. Eventually, I began to feel like a death row prisoner being marched down to the electric chair every time I walked toward the revolving entry door. Once inside, I would transform into an angry slug.

I knew I had to quit when I started fantasizing about poisoning customers. I never thought about stuff like that before, but working at Night Burger did something to my mind. The only place I knew where to get poison was from shoe boxes. Anytime I got a new pair of shoes, a small bag of poison would be sitting inside the box. I never understood why poison was in shoe boxes. Maybe shoe companies hated customers as much as I did and hoped they'd think it was candy or something. I thought about collecting the poison and setting it on the food tray like a salt packet. That way, it would look more like suicide than murder. Luckily for everyone, new shoes cost a lot of money and I needed to save for community college.

"YOU GOT IT! HOLY CRAP! YOU GOT IT!"

Henry didn't say anything. He just smiled and nodded. I reached out to feel the gray leather.

"No!" He slapped my hand away.

"I just want to feel it."

"No touching."

"Why?" I asked.

He stroked the puffy armrests. "This isn't for you."

After Henry got his E-Z-Rest, all he wanted to do was sit around and watch TV. He told me that after all these years, he felt like he could "finally die comfortable." I didn't know why he cared so much about dying comfortable. I would rather live comfortable than die comfortable. My life had actually become pretty *un*comfortable after quitting Night Burger as my mom wasn't too thrilled about me hanging around the house all summer. Whenever we ran into one another, she would say things like "I don't know why you quit that job" or "I hope you don't plan on living here forever."

I tried explaining to her how I needed a break, but she never understood.

"I haven't had a break my entire life," she would say.

I could have told her about the poison stuff, but I didn't want her thinking she'd adopted some psycho. If I adopted some kid and found out they were thinking murderous thoughts, I'd return them. I don't know the exact policies on returning a child, but there has to be some sort of non-psycho guarantee.

Since I didn't have school or work and Henry, who became addicted to late-night TV, didn't wake up until 3 p.m., I spent a good portion of my day watching daytime television, and since I watched daytime television, I quickly became addicted to soap operas. I never thought I'd become a fan of a show that's all about hot tubs and steamy love affairs, but I soon discovered the magic.

The three soaps I watched aired at 11 a.m. (*Seven Days a Week*), 12 p.m. (*Four Seasons*), and 1 p.m. (*Forbidden Fantasy*). My favorite was *Four Seasons*. The show had the craziest twists, most scandalous hookups, and "Oh my!" heartbreaking betrayals. *Seven Days a Week* and *Forbidden Fantasy* were just mediocre in my book. Their characters weren't too believable and the story lines seemed forced. For instance, in one episode of *Forbidden Fantasy*, this guy, Tex, took revenge on his unfaithful wife, Tabitha, by drugging her and putting her in a lion's cage. When Tabitha wakes up, she's inside the cage about to be devoured by the lion. Next thing you know, Gerard, the older and more sophisticated man she's having an affair with, comes to her rescue. Gerard tells the lion about their special bond and ends up talking the savage beast out of viciously attacking his true love. It sounds like a decent idea on paper, but I'm not that stupid.

"I want some goddamn fur!" Henry's mom yelled.

"Not while I'm *alive!*" Henry's dad yelled back.

Henry pointed the remote at the TV and turned up the volume.

"You should move the E-Z-Rest into your bedroom," I suggested.

"I like it out here."

CRASH! Something shattered. "I hate you!" and then "I hate you too!" *LOUD FOOTSTEPS!* The front door opened and slammed shut. I could hear Henry's mom crying in the kitchen.

"I bet you can't wait to leave for college," I said.

"I'm thinking about taking the year off."

"Really?"

"Yeah," Henry replied. "I want to enjoy this E-Z-Rest."

I didn't think Henry passing on his football scholarship to Miracle University was the best idea, but it would keep him in Glenshire and also end his football career.

"Yeah," I said. "Take the year off."

Every weekday, the house phone rang at exactly 10:55 a.m. I'd be sitting on the couch in the living room waiting for *Seven Days a Week* to begin and my mom would bolt out of her bedroom, grab the cordless, run back into her room, and close the door. I never asked her who called, but I assumed it was Ruth.[*]

Halfway through the summer, Henry's dad was killed in a car explosion. It happened at his dad's used car lot, right before a test drive. According to the Glenshire Post, the car

---

[*] Ruth was the mystery woman that my mom talked to on the phone all the time. Whenever they talked, my mom became a happier person.

was leaking some gas and a spark from the ignition caused the car to explode. Henry was devastated. The services were held at the Benzy-Kron Funeral Home. Henry had his E-Z-Rest set right next to the casket. I sat in the back and watched a bunch of well-dressed people I'd never seen before whispering and hugging and crying. I wanted to go up to Henry and shake his hand like everyone else, but I didn't feel like waiting in the long line. As the weeks passed, Henry got worse. He stopped showering, rarely changed his clothes, and started eating lots of junk food. He also started becoming violent. If the smallest thing didn't go his way, he would freak out. This one time, a commercial for Mystery Macaroni came on the TV and he started screaming until he managed to change the channel. Eventually, Henry stopped talking altogether. I tried consoling him, but nothing I said could snap him out of his funk. His mom suggested I give him some space. "He's been through so much," she told me. "He needs time to heal."

I continued watching my soaps during the day, but after that, I had nothing to do. I started taking long bike rides by myself. I pedaled fast through Glenshire and focused my mind on the wind and sky and pavement and handgrips and gears and trees and people and storefronts and anything else outside of me that didn't allow me to look in. Some nights, I rode up to Night Burger. Not to eat, but just to stand outside and stare at the building. Night Burger used to be the greatest restaurant ever. Now I hated it and wanted it gone. I imagined the giant moon exploding and the entire place disappearing into the darkness.

"What are you watching?" asked my mom.

"Nothing," I said as I quickly changed the channel.

"You were watching *Four Seasons*."

I noticed that she didn't have the cordless in her hand. I flipped back.

"It's pretty good."

For the rest of the summer, my mom and I watched all the different soap operas together. She told me how Ruth was traveling overseas and how the cost of talking on the phone every day would be too expensive.

I was glad my mom joined me for the soaps because it was like watching TV with Henry. *Four Seasons* was still the best. We talked about the various story lines and theories we had, who we liked, who we wanted killed off, and which love affairs were the most scandalous. It was the most we ever talked. During commercials, I learned more about Ruth. She and my mom were best friends growing up. They lived down the street from one another and attended the same schools all through high school. They did everything together. Dressed the same, read the same books, liked the same movies, and fell in love with the same boys. It was almost like they were the same person. Growing up, they had this pact that they would always be together, but my mom met my dad and Ruth took a travel job far, far away.

"We used to watch the soaps in person," my mom told me, "but now we watch them together via telephone."

"That's awesome."

My mom loved talking about Ruth and I loved hearing about their wild times. It reminded me of hanging out with Henry. I wanted to tell my mom about all the bike rides and Night Burger adventures we went on as kids but never did.

The week before summer ended, I stopped by Henry's. His mom answered the front door wearing some furry scarf.

"He's in the living room," she said.

Henry was sitting on his E-Z-Rest watching TV. I walked over and sat on the couch.

"Hey," I said.

He had a decent-sized beard, and his brown hair hung just below his eyebrows. He looked like Peter from *Four Seasons* after spending three months in prison for a crime he didn't commit.

"How's everything going?"

Henry didn't say anything.

"I start community college next week."

No response.

"I still have to get my notebooks, folders, pens, and all that," I told him. "I got a car. It's a 1984 LaPree. I bought it off this guy that my da—" I stopped myself before I said it.

We sat in silence.

"You want to go to Night Burger?"

Henry shook is head.

"You still taking the year off college?"

Henry nodded.

I thought about my mom and Ruth and their pact to stick together.

"You should take classes at Token with me," I said.

Henry shook his head.

"Why not?"

He grabbed the wooden E-Z-Rest handle and reclined. "College isn't this comfortable."

The next day, I opened my dresser drawer and pulled out the letter with no return address. I sat at the edge of my bed and thought about Sam from *Quantum* and how much opening the letter had changed his life. I thought about who could have sent it, but no one came to mind. The only thing I could think of was that maybe the police tapped into my thoughts somehow and found out about all that poison stuff. But why would they send a letter? *Wouldn't they just kick down the door and arrest me?*

Eventually I came to the conclusion that this was my last week as a kid. I started community college on Monday. It was time I start taking responsibility for my life and acting like a man. I opened the envelope and pulled out a white piece of notebook paper. It was dated June 4, 1993, and read:

Dear Tom,

I am your real mother, Jane Mitchell. I want you to know how proud I am of you and all your achievements.

Congratulations on graduating high school! I wish I could have been there for you. You were the most beautiful baby boy. I wish I could explain everything to you. I wasn't ready to be a mother. I think about you every day. I understand if you don't want anything to do with me. You are not to blame for any of this. I named you after my father.

I love you very much.

~ Jane

The letter was short and didn't explain much. I already knew I was adopted. My fake parents told me early on, so things didn't get weird in the later years. There was an address on the bottom of the page. I didn't know why she told me about naming me after her father. I don't like when first names travel down the family tree. I'm sure it's distracting when there are twenty Toms at the same family party.

I put the letter back in the envelope and tossed it inside my dresser drawer. *Four Seasons* was about to begin.

seventeen

*T*O WHOM *It May Concern:*

Tom Mitchell has a severe panda allergy. Exposure to panda causes his throat to swell making it difficult for him to breathe. Panda contact also makes his skin itch and eyes water. He should avoid panda at all costs.

Dr. Edward V. Venkin

The last time I visited Henry's mom's house, she said she would call the police if I ever returned without a doctor's note explaining my panda allergy. I've never faked a doctor's note before, but I feel pretty confident about this one. It sounds professional. I also used my left hand to write it so it looks like a real doctor's handwriting. All doctors have bad handwriting. They're too busy saving lives with their hands and don't have time to write neatly. Whenever doctors have to write, they're saying to themselves, "I could be unclogging a heart right now!" or something like that.

The front door opens. Henry's mom's entire body is covered in fur.

"Hello," I say.

"Get off my property," she demands.

"I—"

"I'm calling the cops."

"Wait!" I shout. "I have a doctor's note!"

"Hand it over."

I place the note in her furry hand. She holds it up to her furry eyeholes, reads it, and hands it back. "You have three minutes."

"I'm only here to talk about Henry."

"What about my Henry?" she asks. "Is he okay?"

"Yeah, he's fine."

She places her furry hand on her furry chest. "Don't scare me like that."

"Sorry," I say. "Anyway, he misses you very much."

"Really?"

"Oh, yeah. He wants to see you, but he thinks you don't want to see him."

"That's not true."

"That's what I told him, but he won't listen."

She crosses her furry arms. "He gets that from his dead father."

"If you're not doing anything today, he's working, if you want to stop by."

"Henry has a job?"

"He works with me at Rudy's Grocery."

"Out in Cary?"

"Yep."

"Why so far away?"

"It's not important. What is important is you and Henry. You miss him, and he misses you. Go to Rudy's."

"You think that's a good idea?"

"Definitely."

I fill her in on all the details (directions, work schedule, etc.) and repeat over and over how much Henry misses her.

"Thanks, Tom," she says. "Henry's lucky to have you as a friend."

⊜ ⊜ ⊜

As I'm about to leave, Henry's mom asks what I think about her new zebra yard (I forgot to mention that all the green grass surrounding Henry's mom's house has been removed and converted to zebra).

"I like it."

"The best part is that it's maintenance-free."

"So you don't have to mow it or anything?" I ask.

"Exactly."

"Nice," I say. "That's a great outfit too."

"Thanks!" she replies. "The gloves are fox, the boots bobcat, the pants elk, the coat snow leopard, and the mask is made from a variety of monkeys."

"Looks terrific," I say. "You should wear that when you visit Henry."

She nods. "I will."

I walk down the furry steps back to my LaPree.

"Oh, and Tom . . ."

I look back. "Yeah?"

"Sorry for questioning your panda allergy."

"It's okay," I say. "Happens all the time."

Back at the apartment, I sit on the blue couch and think about how everything got so screwed up between Henry and me. I alter the past by changing important details and discover how much better my life would have been if I'd never:

- Worked at Night Burger . . .
- Told Henry about Rudy's . . .
- Lied . . .

I imagine all sorts of "If I'd never" scenarios until the VCR clock reads 12 a.m., at which point I roll off the blue couch and sit on the E-Z-Rest carpet circle, staring at the front door. Any second now, Henry will enter, his eyes filled with tears.

"They hate me, Tom," he'll say.

"Don't worry," I'll tell him. "You don't need those stupid High School and College Kids anyway."

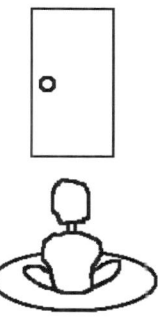

I wake up the next morning curled up on the E-Z-Rest carpet circle. I must have fallen asleep last night. "Henry?" I call out. No response. His mom must have never made it to Rudy's. I get to my feet and walk into the kitchen. A handwritten note sits on the counter:

Dear Tom,

Fuck you.

Henry

P.S. I will be stopping by this Friday after work to pick up my belongings and move out for good.

eighteen

I PULLED the Token Village Community College newspaper from my backpack and spread it out on the hallway
bench.

"Excuse me," someone said.

I looked up and saw a girl standing there. She had
brown hair and glasses and wore an ugly green dress.

"What are you reading?" she asked.

My first thought was that it was pretty obvious what I
was reading. "The paper," I said.

"Anything good?"

"No."

She held out her hand. "I'm Cassie."

"Tom."

We shook hands. I didn't know what she was doing. I wanted her to leave so I could pretend to read and eat my lunch in the hallway by myself like I always did.

"Can I sit down?" she asked.

I hesitated.

"I don't have to."

I collected the newspaper pages and shoved them inside my backpack.

"Thanks!"

She opened her purse and pulled out a sandwich wrapped in plastic. "Aren't you going to eat?" she asked.

"No," I said. "I'm not hungry."

"You like peanut butter and jelly?"

"Not really."

"Everyone likes peanut butter and jelly."

"I don't."

"Have you had it with Villayne's Peanut Butter?"

"I'm not sure," I said. "My mom does the shopping."

She took a bite of her sandwich. "Mmm, it's so good. You want some?"

"No, thanks."

"Here." She ripped off a piece and held it toward me. "Try it."

"I can't."

"It's only a small piece."

I wasn't in the mood to be arguing over peanut butter and jelly, so I grabbed the piece of sandwich and popped it in my mouth. Cassie smiled.

"So?"

I chewed and swallowed. "It's good."

Cassie and I began eating lunch together after that. She was pretty easy to talk to and didn't mind eating lunch in the hallway.

"I would eat in the cafeteria," I told her, "but I have sensitive hearing."

"Aw," she said. "Poor baby."

Cassie was sweet and caring and loved helping people, which explained why she was studying to become a nurse.

"What about you, Tom?" she asked. "What are you studying?"

I didn't want her knowing I was undecided, so I said the first thing that came to mind. "Business."

Her green eyes lit up. "Wow, business. You must be real smart."

I wasn't. In fact, I was a C student.

"What are your classes like?" she asked.

The only thing I knew about business was from working at Night Burger, so whenever Cassie asked me anything business-related, I just pretty much swapped out the words *Night Burger* with *Business World*.

"Customers are number one in the Business World."

"Business World employees love talking behind each other's backs."

"The Business World needs to be clean and organized."

I never planned on lying to Cassie about my sensitive hearing and field of study, but it sort of just happened. I wanted to tell her the truth about everything, but I couldn't take back everything I said and start over. She would leave the hallway bench and never trust me again. I didn't want that. She was nice, fun, and most importantly, helped me forget about Henry.

A few weeks before spring semester ended, Cassie asked me to be her boyfriend. I'd never had a girlfriend before, so I told her I'd think about it.

"Forget it, then," she said.

"What?" I asked.

"You'll *think* about it?!"

"Yeah."

She turned her back to me and took a bite of her peanut butter and jelly sandwich.

"Do you like me, Tom?" she eventually asked.

"Yes."

"Then why didn't you say yes?"

"I don't know," I said. "I've never had a girlfriend and wanted some time to think about what that means."

She leaned in and kissed me on the lips.

"That's what it means," she said.

"Okay, then."

I wasn't too excited about summer vacation. My fake dad got me a job at Teltrox and Cassie was going away to her parents' lake house. She invited me along, but I needed to work so I had money to pay for my second year of community college. She told me that she'd call me every night and come home every other weekend. It wasn't the ideal situation, but there was nothing I could do.

My fake dad woke me up early Monday morning. "Time to get up, Tom." I got dressed and ate some Magic O's cereal. By 6:30, we were out the door and driving to work in my fake dad's Delco pickup truck. Some talk radio station was playing over the speakers. *"Sixty degrees in Dire, sixty-three in Cary, sixty-one in Token Village, sixty in Glenshire . . ."* I stared out the window and watched the houses and trees blur past. I had never been inside Teltrox before. I'd only seen it from the outside. It was a giant, square, metal factory building with no windows or anything. Henry and I used to ride our bikes past it when we were still friends. We called this area The Fields because there were cornfields surrounding the building.

The inside of Teltrox looked like a small city. The ceiling was super high and the building stretched out in all directions. The entire place was lit up with long ceiling lights that ran up and down the factory. Set up throughout were giant machines moving and flashing and making all sorts of noise. Men wearing yellow hard hats walked around and yelled to one another.

"The stretch coating's off!"

"More oil in the fabric tester!"

"We're not dealing with socks here, boys!"

I was assigned to one of the observation stations and in charge of removing faulty pantyhose. I stared at the thin elongated tubes as they slowly moved along the conveyer belt and entered the Checking Box. If the pantyhose were free of defects, the conveyer belt moved forward. If defects were detected, this loud buzzing sound went off and I had to open the Checking Box, remove the faulty pantyhose, and toss them in this red plastic bin. I then had to push this green button to resume operation.

The entire factory shut down for lunch. All the machines stopped working and the small city went quiet. I removed my yellow hard hat and earplugs. Everyone started walking in the same direction. I followed the crowd and entered a cafeteria. "Tom!" My fake dad waved me over. He was sitting at a table with some guys.

"Have a seat," my fake dad said. "I'll grab us some food."

While he was gone, I met Donny, Ron, Carl, Eddie, Rick, Steve, and Frankie.

"So, Tommy," said Ron. "Whatcha studyin' in school?"

"Oh . . . I'm actually undecided."

"Figure it out soon," he warned. "You don't wanna end up workin' here your whole life."

All the guys laughed.

My fake dad returned with two Monday specials—meat loaf, potatoes and gravy, corn, and a pop. I ate in silence while all the guys talked about work, news, and weather.

"Hotter than a pistol this morning."

"Supposed to be in the nineties all week."

"You all hear about that mother and daughter who were killed in that car accident?"

"Goddamn shame."

"Tragic."

"I'll tell you what's tragic: working at Teltrox."

The overhead alarm sounded. *WAH! WAH! WAH!* All the guys stood up, put on their yellow hard hats, inserted their earplugs, and went back to work. The machines fired up and the small city came to life. I returned to the observation station and worked until the alarm sounded again at 5 p.m. After that, we disinfected our hard hats, threw our earplugs in the trash, and clocked out.

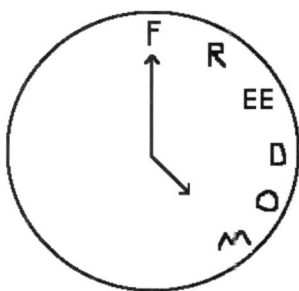

"I hate it," I told Cassie over the phone that night. "It's so *loud*, and all I do is stand and stare at pantyhose all day."

"Aw," she said. "I'm sorry."

"I have to wear earplugs and a yellow hard hat." I kept complaining. "It's hot . . . makes me tired . . . wake up at 6 a.m."

Cassie told me not to worry because it was only a summer job. Easy for her to say, considering she was spending her summer at a lake house where all she had to worry about was swimming and cruising on boats all day.

"I have to go," I said. "I'm starting to fall asleep."

"Have a good day tomorrow," she said. "Miss you."

"Miss you too."

"Miss you more."

"Miss you most."

The summer dragged on. Working at Teltrox slowed everything down. I'd never worked such a boring job. The only decent part was not having to deal with customers. I didn't even think about poisoning them anymore; I just thought about poisoning myself. I didn't understand how my fake dad worked there every day. The job took everything out of you. It took your spirit, your energy, and your ability to think. I now understood why my fake dad never said much whenever he was home. His mind was too numb from working. All he could do was eat, watch TV, and sleep. Talking took too much effort. I tried explaining this talking problem to Cassie, hoping we could cut our nightly phone calls down from an hour to thirty minutes, but she told me that boyfriends should want to talk to their girlfriends.

"It's not that I don't want to talk to you," I said. "It's just that I can't think after working all day."

"Well, you're not thinking on the phone—you're talk-ing."

"I know, but I have to think about what to talk about."

"It doesn't matter what we talk about," she said. "I just want to hear your voice."

Every other weekend, Cassie would drive home to her parents' house in Token Village. We spent our time together hanging out at her place, talking, watching TV, and making out. Her parents were never home. They stayed at the lake house all summer. It was nice not having to deal with any more adults. Working at Night Burger and Teltrox made me realize that I didn't have much in common with them.

Ⓢ Ⓢ Ⓢ

"What's your life's dream?" Cassie asked me one night.

"What do you mean?"

She muted the television and sat facing me on the couch. "My life's dream is to travel the world and help someone in every country."

"Nice."

"What about you?" she asked. "What's your life's dream?"

I really didn't have any dreams.

"So?"

"Own a business one day."

"What type of business?"

I said the first thing that came to mind. "Restaurant."

"What type of restaurant?"

"Fast food."

"What would you call it?"

"Ah . . . Night Burger."

The weekend before fall semester started, Cassie asked me if I wanted to have sex.

"Sure."

We drove over to U-Pump Gas Station to pick up some condoms. I handed her five dollars and asked her to go inside and buy them.

"Why do I have to go?" she asked.

"It will be easier that way."

"That doesn't make any sense."

"I just don't want any trouble."

She opened the car door and left. I sat in the driver's seat and watched her through the windshield. She was in and out in less than a minute. The car door opened.

"Here," she said as she threw the package at me.

"Thanks."

She closed the door and put her seatbelt on. "Just drive."

We got back to Cassie's parents' place shortly after and went straight to her bedroom. She lit some candles and turned off all the lights. We didn't talk or anything. We went right into kissing, and next thing I know, we're naked and having sex on her bed. All three condoms were used up in an hour.

☰ ☰ ☰

Summer ended and school began. I couldn't be happier. I didn't have to work at Teltrox anymore, and Cassie and I were in love.

"I think it's time I meet your parents," she told me while walking to class.

"Why?" I asked.

"Tom, we've been dating for almost six months now," she said. "I haven't even been to your house."

"I already told you, there's nothing to do over there."

We stopped outside of Cassie's classroom door. "I'm coming over on Saturday."

"But—"

"No buts." She kissed me on the lips. "Love you."

"Love you, too."

☰ ☰ ☰

On Saturday, I called Cassie and told her my parents were out to dinner. The following Saturday, I told her they were ill. The Saturday after that, I told her they were on vacation.

"This is ridiculous!" she exclaimed. "I want to meet your parents!"

"You will," I assured her.

"When?" she asked. "I've been trying to for three weeks now."

We sat on the hallway bench in silence.

"I think you're hiding something from me," she said.

I looked away. "No."

Cassie took a bite of her peanut butter and jelly sandwich. "I think we should start eating in the cafeteria."

"Why?" I asked.

"I don't want to eat lunch in the hallway anymore."

"The cafeteria's too loud."

"It's not that loud," she replied.

"But I have sensitive hearing."

"Look," she said. "If I meet your parents this weekend, we'll continue to eat in the hallway. If not, we're eating in the cafeteria."

The weekend came and went. Cassie never met my fake parents. "Sorry," I told her over the phone, "they—"

"Fine!" she snapped. "But we're done eating lunch on that stupid bench!"

"We'll see."

I avoided Cassie all Monday morning. She caught up with me during lunch. I was sitting on the hallway bench.

"What are you doing here?" she asked. "We're supposed to eat in the cafeteria."

"Sorry," I said. "I can't."

Cassie stormed off.

From that moment on, our relationship transformed from one of love into one of hate. We stopped holding hands and talking on the phone and hanging out and having sex and saying "I love you" and started hating one another.

"You're stubborn," she said.

"You're needy," I said.

We had both given everything we could to the relationship, and there was nothing left. Cassie hated me and I hated her. I don't know why she continued to eat lunch in the hallway with me, considering that eating in the cafeteria was so important to her. I wished she would leave. I wished she didn't exist. I wished I could travel back in time to when we first met and never taste that stupid peanut butter and jelly sandwich.

🍔 🍔 🍔

"You remind me of my ex-boyfriend," Cassie said during lunch one day.

"Yeah, why's that?" I asked.

"He was a liar."

"I never lied to you."

"I can't even look at you anymore."

"Then don't."

We turned our backs to one another and bit into our respected sandwiches.

"I should have never dated you," she eventually said. "I knew it wasn't right."

"Then why did you date me?"

"I felt sorry for you, sitting in the hallway eating lunch by yourself. It was pathetic."

"You're pathetic."

"Great comeback, Tom."

"I never asked you to eat lunch with me," I said. "I was fine on my own."

"*HA!*"

"What's so funny?"

"You'll never be fine on your own," she said. "You wouldn't know what to do with yourself."

I didn't need her. I didn't need anyone.

"Yeah," I said. "Well, guess what, I'm a C student!"

"What?"

"I'm not smart," I said. "I told you I was, but I'm not."

"I *knew* you were a *liar*."

She stood up. I stood up too.

"And one more thing!" I yelled. "I'm not even a business major. I'm undecided! You hear that? You were dating someone who was *undecided!*"

"You're insane."

"I'll tell you what's insane. You and your stupid life's dream! You can't help someone in every country. I checked into it, and there are way too many countries and traveling to each one would cost way too much money!"

Cassie's face turned bright red and a single tear slid down her cheek. Everyone in the hallway was staring at us. I immediately wanted to take back everything I said, but it was too late. There was nothing I could say or do to make things better.

I grabbed my backpack and took off.

nineteen

The three main employee groups are no longer talking to me. They ignore me on the grocery floor and act like I don't exist. I know what they're doing. They've delivered their threats, and now they're sitting back and watching me suffer. People love watching others suffer. It makes them feel better about themselves: "At least my life's not as bad as that guy's." It's the way people are programmed. I'm the same way. I wish there were another Tom Mitchell who I could watch. Horrible life. No friends. Mixed up in the head. I'd love to watch that.

"Excuse me," someone says. I deflate and turn around. A customer stands holding two oranges, one in each hand. "Look at these oranges!" he says. "They're huge!" I don't know what this guy expects me to say. "Oh, my! You're right! These oranges are *huge!*" Then what? We talk oranges for twenty minutes. I have Farm Fresh Potatoes to stock. I don't have time for big orange conversations. I'm tired of the pointless conversations, the questions, the attitudes, the assholes, the idiots, the big-orange talkers, the where's-the-bathrooms, the can-I-get-a-discounts, the talk-to-mes, the help-mes, the where-is-everythings, the get-your-managers, the complainers, the destroyers, the yellers, the ruiners, the customers.

Henry now wears a gold crown and enters Rudy's on a red carpet that the High School and College Kids roll out for him. I thought having his mom show up to work would ruin his image (since all High School and College Kids care about is image) but that wasn't the case. If anything, Henry's screwed-up mom has made him more of a High School and College Kid than ever before. "It's cool," they probably said after meeting his furry mom. "Our parents are screwed-up too." If Henry's mom were a normal furless adult, *then* the High School and College Kids would have kicked him out of their group and he would have apologized to me and protected me from all this war nonsense, but now, Henry is King of the High School and College Kids and rumor on the grocery floor is that he wants my head.

Pete calls me into the office and tells me that he needs me to make a sign that reads: *Open 24/7, 365.*

"I want it BIG on the storefront windows."

"Why?" I ask.

"The Rudy's grand re-opening."

"When's that?"

"Kicks off this Saturday," he says. "Where ya been?"

He hands me a clear plastic bag filled with construction paper, markers, scissors, and tape.

"So you want me to make a sign that reads: Open 24/7, 365?"

"YES!" Pete shouts. "How many times I gotta say it?"

"Aren't we already open 24/7, 365?"

Pete slaps his hand against his forehead. "You're missing the point, Mitchell," he says. "People like to *see* things."

Working on the sign allows me to watch Lisa all afternoon. She looks extra pretty today and has her brown hair pulled back in a ponytail. I love the way she slides the grocery items over the built-in barcode scanner. She's definitely my type of woman. I'm probably going to have to join the Voyeurs. If Lisa ever found out about my employee voyeurism, the wedding would definitely be off.

"Keep driving," I say. "Nothing illegal going on here."

There's a cop tailing me. I think he knows about the stolen toilet paper inside my trunk.

"Unit twenty to dispatch," he's probably radioing in. "I'm heading southbound on Davis Street following a gray LaPree. Send backup. Over."

I drive the speed limit and obey all traffic signs. If the red and blue lights start flashing, I'm slamming my foot on the gas. No way am I going to prison.

I lie on my air mattress and picture myself dying alone on a hospital bed. I shorten my breath and feel my internal organs shut down one by one. I silently say good-bye to myself as I turn off my brain and imagine what nothing is like.

Wednesday

I park. Exit car. Zip up sweatshirt. Walk across parking lot. Enter Rudy's. Clock in. Office. Pete. Stock list. Grocery floor. Break room. Lock up sweatshirt. Grocery floor. Back room. *Knock, knock, knock.* Get stock. Stock shelves. Help customers. "TOM MITCHELL OUT FOR CARTS. TOM MITCHELL OUT FOR CARTS." Break room. Sweatshirt. Toilet paper. Exit store. Car. Open trunk. Insert toilet paper roll. Gather carts. Enter Rudy's. Grocery floor. Break room. Lock up sweatshirt. Grocery floor. Repeat, repeat, repeat. It's the same horrible thing over and over. I don't know how people do it. The routine of working at Rudy's is enough to drive someone mad. I'm going to have to work this job my entire life. I don't know what my real parents were thinking when they created me. I doubt my real mom and dad were space adventurers or anything cool like that.

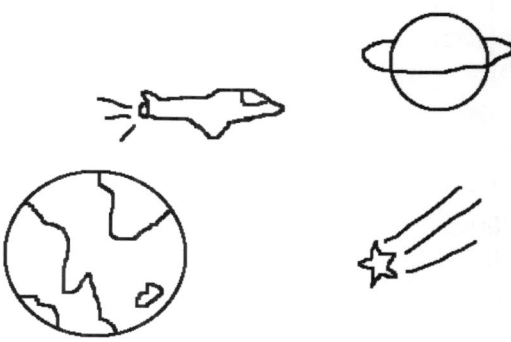

The streets are empty. No cops. No cars. No people. I drive home with my window down and let the steady howl of the air drown my thoughts. "Help me!" thousands of little thoughts scream as they fight to stay alive in my head. "Help me!"

⊜ ⊜ ⊜

I open my bedroom closet, grab the Mr. Jim's Life Improvement Kit box, and call the customer service number.

"Thank you for calling Mr. Jim's Life Improvement Kit customer service center, Mr. Erik speaking."

"I'd like a refund," I say.

"Excuse me, sir?"

"I'd like a refund," I repeat.

"Are you a current customer?"

"Yes."

"May I have your name?"

"Mitchell," I say. "Tom Mitchell."

"Let me pull up your account." Pause. "Okay, Mr. Mitchell, how can I help you?"

I explain how I bought the Life Improvement Kit a few months back and how it didn't solve any of my problems.

"I'm sorry for your dissatisfaction," Mr. Erik says. "The kit's results can vary from person to person; however, the kit typically has a ninety-nine percent success rate."

"Well, it didn't work for me," I tell him. "In fact, it ruined my relationship with my best friend and in two days he'll be moving out for good and I work a crappy job and don't make enough money to live on my own so I need some extra cash and since this dumb kit didn't work, I want a refund."

"I'm sorry," he says, "but you no longer qualify for the thirty-day money-back guarantee."

"I'd like to speak to the manager."

Mr. Erik puts me on hold. There's a recording of Mr. Jim's voice playing. *"Don't think about your problems and they will disappear. Take a deep breath and clear your mind. One Don't Think Push-up. Two. Three. I hold the solutions, I hold the answers, I hold the secrets to living a great life—"*

The recording cuts out.

"Mr. Jim's Life Improvement Kit customer service center, Ms. Barb speaking."

"Hello, Ms. Barb." I explain the situation to her, just as I explained it to Mr. Erik. "I just want my money back. The kit didn't work for me."

"I apologize, Mr. Mitchell, but according to your account, you've had the kit more than thirty days so the money-back guarantee no longer applies."

"Why not?"

"We're not authorized to offer refunds after the initial thirty-day period."

"Why?"

"Because our return policy is only valid for thirty days."

"Why?"

"Mr. Mitchell, the policy was clearly stated on the infomercial as well as the pamphlet included with your kit."

"Well," I say, "I *did* write a refund request letter a few days after I got the kit and never got a response."

"Where did you send the letter?" Ms. Barb asks.

"The address on the box the kit came in."

"I'm sorry, but that's the address of our manufacturing plant. You should have called if you were unsatisfied."

"I didn't feel like talking to anyone."

"I'm sorry for your trouble, Mr. Mitchell, but again, there's nothing we can do."

"Fuck you! Idiot! *Asshole!*"

I hang up the phone and go to bed.

Thursday

The big orange Rudy's sign is being taken down by these guys in yellow hard hats. The *R*, *u*, and *d* have already been removed. It just says *y's Grocery*. They must be changing the name for the grand re-opening.

"ATTENTION, RUDY'S CUSTOMERS! STARTING THIS SATURDAY, RUDY'S WILL BE CELEBRATING ITS GRAND RE-OPENING! ONCE AGAIN, STARTING THIS SATURDAY, RUDY'S WILL BE CELEBRATING ITS GRAND RE-OPENING!"

Pete's unsatisfied with my *Open 24/7, 365* sign progress and tells me to "Pick up the pace." I tell him "I'm working as fast as I can." He tells me "Work faster!" I hate managers. They think every job takes two seconds. I'd be done a long time ago if I didn't have to deal with stock, customers, carts, recovery, bagging, and everything else. Nothing is ever good enough for Pete. He's great at making employees feel even more worthless than they already do. I hate managers. If I moved into a new home and my neighbor were a manager, I'd move again. If I got married and had a daughter and she wanted to marry a manager, I wouldn't allow it. If I walked into a movie theater and there was a scene with a manager, I would leave my seat, walk to the box office, ask for the manager, and start throwing my popcorn and yelling, "I don't want to see you *manager people* in my movies!"

Henry's a train conductor flying down the tracks. His head sticks out the side window. He pulls the hanging wire that sounds the horn. *TOOT! TOOT!* I'm tied to the steel tracks like in the cartoons. I can't move. The vibrations rattle my body. The train nears. I struggle to break free. *TOOT! TOOT!* Closer. Louder. I see Henry's face. His hair's flying all over and he's laughing like a maniac. He thinks it's funny that I can't move. He has me just where he wants me. I twist and turn but it's no use. I give up. The back of my head hits the ground and I look up toward the blue sky. The vibrations increase. Closer. Closer. Louder. Louder. *TOOT! TOOT!* Henry plows the train directly through me. I die. I won't describe what my dead body looks like because it's pretty disgusting.

I push my cart of go-backs* up and down the various aisles. I hate go-backs. Every shift, there are carts and carts of them. In a perfect world, go-backs wouldn't exist, but in this world, customers love tossing grocery items where they don't belong. "I don't want these pickles anymore, but I'm not in the pickle aisle. Oh, well, I'll put the pickles with the soup." I've seen customers in their fifties, sixties, seventies and even eighties put items back where they don't belong. These people have been living life for years and years and still don't understand how things work. I would love to educate these customers on the art of putting items back where they belong, but I'm not allowed to say anything at Rudy's.

"You're fired, Mitchell!" Pete would say.

"Why?"

"For telling that customer to put the pickles back with the pickles."

"She put the pickles in the soup aisle," I'd say. "Pickles don't go in the soup aisle."

"Then ya wait till she leaves and ya put it back."

"She should put it back!"

"She's the customer! Customers do what they want!"

I'm sick of companies allowing customers the freedom to do and say whatever they want yet punishing employees for doing and saying *anything* they want. I can't keep playing this fake employee role. Rudy's isn't a grocery store; it's a mental prison, and Pete is the warden. At least, in regular prison, people can *say* what they want. Here in the outside

---

* A go-back is any misplaced grocery item that needs to go back to its original location.

world, we live these fake lives and pretend to be these friendly employees. We dress a certain way, wear name tags, and follow ridiculous orders for no real purpose. This is the life we *choose* to live. I'm not signing up for it. Put me in handcuffs! Lock me away! I don't know what I was thinking when that cop was tailing me on Tuesday. I'd love to go to prison. I can be myself. Talk how I want to talk. It sucks that I won't be able to leave when I want, but I'll take the mental freedom over the physical. I don't do much anyway. I work this job and sit in my apartment. That's my life.

"ARREST ME!" I scream. "I HAVE A TRUCK FULL OF STOLEN TOILET PAPER!"

There's a cop tailing me again. I'm flying down Davis Street and breaking every traffic law. The red and blue lights won't go on. I roll down my window and yell, "*I'M A CRIMINALLL!!!*"

Nothing.

I lie on my air mattress, unable to sleep. I try to think about nothing, but nothing turns into everything. My head feels dizzy. I don't know what to do. I'm becoming angry at everything. Before work today, I started yelling at my comb for not combing my hair right. *"Fuck you, comb!"* I yelled and yelled and threw the comb all over the apartment. I eventually snapped it in half. It's stupid. I'm attacking things that don't matter. I should attack Henry, but attacking people is against my No-Bother Policy. Everything's against my No-Bother Policy. I can't even talk to people! Not that I want to talk to people. I was happy talking with Henry—the old Henry. The new Henry's an asshole. Short hair. Healthy. Popular. Thinking about him makes me want to kill myself. Everyone says that suicide's a permanent solution to a temporary problem, but I think that suicide's a permanent solution to a permanent problem. Saying *temporary* is an assumption. People assume everything. No one really knows what anyone else is going through. People act like they do, but they don't. "Oh, I'm so sorry. It's okay. Everything will be fine." Not every problem can be fixed with a few words or whatever. I'm twenty-six years old. People think I'm in my mid-thirties. I never met my real parents. My fake parents are dead. Every year gets worse. I only needed one friend my entire life. That's all. One person to understand me and talk to me. The war is now two days away. I should just join one of the stupid groups and go out fighting. I don't care if I live or die anymore. At least if I die fighting, I'll be remembered as a war hero.

twenty

I FAKED SICK the rest of the week. I never wanted to set foot inside Token Village Community College ever again. I didn't want to see Cassie, the students, the teachers, or even the creepy janitor. I'm sure the entire school was talking about what happened.

"You hear about that Tom Mitchell kid, who was fighting with his girlfriend?"

"Of course."

"Supposedly he was lying about being this hotshot business major."

"I heard he was lying about a lot more than that."

College students love talking about fights. It's pretty much all they're interested in. Science, math, English—forget it. There should be a course called Fights. No student would ever skip it. Everyone would get an A.

"What are you studying?"

"Fights. What about you?"

"I'm studying Fights as well."

Eventually, Fights will become the only major offered in college. Everyone will become fight experts. Every job, every relationship, everything will revolve around fights.

"Are you going to school today?" asked my fake mom.

"I still don't feel well."

"You haven't felt well in over a week."

"It won't go away."

She sat on the edge of my bed and placed her hand against my forehead. "You don't have a fever."

"It's my stomach," I said.

"Diarrhea?"

"No."

"Stomach flu?"

"No."

"Then what, Tom?"

"It just hurts."

The phone rang every weekday morning at 10:55 a.m. I assumed it was Ruth calling to chat and watch soap operas via telephone with my fake mom. I thought about getting back into soaps, but I didn't think I deserved it. I didn't deserve to watch TV, ride my bike, eat at Night Burger, or do anything fun. I spent my time locked in my bedroom thinking about Cassie and how I never should have lied to her or told her how her life's dream was stupid. I wanted to call her and tell her I was sorry and that I missed her caring voice, her strange outfits, her flowery smell, her everything, but I never did. Some nights, I would lie awake, staring teary-eyed into the darkness, and whisper *love* messages like:

"Hey, Cassie. It's me, Tom. How are you? I'm okay. Just lying in bed. I miss you."

She never responded.

The weeks passed. I continued faking sick. My fake mom was getting more and more suspicious.

"He's not sick," I overheard her say one night.

"Something's wrong," replied my fake dad.

"I knew this would happen."

"Not so loud."

"We're going to be stuck with him forever."

I began imagining Cassie with other guys. Talking to them. Kissing them. Walking up to them and asking if they liked peanut butter and jelly sandwiches.

"Are you ever going back to school?" my fake mom asked during dinner.

"Probably," I said. "But I need to get healthy first."

"*Liar!*" She grabbed her steak knife and pointed it at me.

My fake dad lunged across the table and grabbed her threatening hand.

"He's not sick!" my fake mom shouted.

"Drop the knife," said my fake dad.

She released her grip. The knife fell onto the kitchen table.

"I'm sorry," she said. "But you need to go back to school, Tom."

"Your mother's right," said my fake dad.

I stared at my mashed potatoes and moved them around with my fork. No way was I ever going back to TVCC. My fake mom would have to kill me first.

I saw Cassie's wedding, met her children, and watched her life continue on without me. Less than three months ago, we were in love, and now we didn't even talk to one another. We were complete strangers. Enemies. I laid on my bed in the dark and whispered *hate* messages like:

"I can't believe you married him!"

She didn't answer.

"And you have children!"

Nothing.

"You broke my heart!"

To take my mind off Cassie's perfect imaginary life, I started doing various activities around my bedroom. I rearranged furniture. Organized dresser drawers. Cleaned out my closet. Anything that occupied my mind and passed the time. Eventually I decided to remove my bedroom wallpaper.

My fake dad brought me into the garage and gave me a bucket, a paint scraper, a step stool, and an old rag. He told me to fill the bucket with warm water, wet the rag, soak the walls to loosen the glue, and use the scraper to scrape the wallpaper off.

"Got it," I said. "Thanks."

"Hey, Tom," said my fake dad. "I've noticed that girl doesn't call anymore."

"Oh." I grabbed the bucket and step stool. "She moved."

"Sorry to hear that."

"Yeah."

"If you ever want to talk—"

"Sure."

I opened the door and walked inside.

The next morning, I moved all my furniture to the center of my bedroom so I could access the walls. I then filled the plastic bucket with warm water, wet the rag, and went to work on the gray elephant themed wallpaper that had surrounded me since I was a kid. I didn't think about anything while I soaked and scraped the walls. The removal took three days—mostly due to the fact that scraping off the wallpaper proved to be a real fight. When everything was finished, I stood in the middle of my room and stared at the walls. The thick paper that covered and protected them all these years was now gone.

KNOCK! KNOCK! KNOCK!

"Tom, phone!"

I wrapped my blanket around my body and hurried to the door.

"Be quick," my fake mom said. "Ruth will be calling soon."

I took the cordless from her and closed the door.

"Hello."

"Hey, Tom," the voice replied.

"Henry?"

twenty-one

THE INSIDE of Forever Furniture is packed with beds, tables, couches, desks, chairs, and so on.

"Can I help you find anything, sir?"

Behind me stands a fat guy with a bad toupee. He looks like Mr. Jim, except instead of a white T-shirt that says **MR. JIM**, he's wearing a brown collared shirt with an *FF* logo and a name tag that reads *Jim*.

"No, thanks," I say.

"If you need anything," he smiles, "let me know."

I enter the recliner section and browse the E-Z-Rests. They have every color except gray. Jim appears. "Find what you're searching for?" he asks.

"No."

"I hold the solutions. I hold the answers. I hold the secrets to living a great life."

"What?"

"*I said*, how can I help you?"

"I need a gray E-Z-Rest."

Jim looks around. "Appears we're all out of gray E-Z-Rests," he says. "We have other gray recliners. Follow me."

"It must be an E-Z-Rest," I state. "If it's not an E-Z-Rest, it's not a real recliner."

"Indeed." He removes his toupee and scratches his bald head. "I'll be right back."

As soon as he leaves, I browse the other gray name-brand recliners—Tenline, Vertical Export, Regal. They look pretty much the same as the E-Z-Rests. They're lower in price, too. I want to believe that buying something besides a gray E-Z-Rest will work for the reenactment I have planned, but I know how particular Henry is about his recliners and how reenactments typically need to be exact in order to work.

≋ ≋ ≋

"Sir!" Jim runs up, out of breath. "I spoke . . . to the manager . . . and we can get you . . . a brand-new . . . gray E-Z-Rest . . . this Monday. All I need . . . is for you to . . . fill out these order forms."

He holds up this giant packet of papers and keels over, gasping for air.

"I need the recliner today."

Jim composes himself. "It's just three days."

"I'm sorry," I say. "But I need it today."

"Sir, it will be here Monday."

"Stop calling me *sir!*"

"Excuse me?"

"I want you to stop calling me sir."

"My apologies," he says. "Sir is how we address our adult male customers."

"How old am I?" I ask.

"Excuse me?"

"How old am I?" I repeat.

Jim looks me over. "Um, I would say thirty—"

"TWENTY-SIX!"

I rip the order forms from his hands and began swatting him with them.

"TWENTY-SIX!" I yell. "TWENTY-SIX!"

He tries shielding his face with his hands, but it's no use.

"TWENTY-SIX! YOUR DUMB KIT DIDN'T WORK! TWENTY-SIX! I WANT A REFUND! TWENTY-SIX! MY LIFE IS WORSE THAN EVER!"

Jim trips and falls to the floor. Blood drips from his left pinky finger.

"You gave me a paper cut," he says.

I toss the order forms into the air and run past customers, employees, and furniture until I burst through the entrance doors, escape to my LaPree, and peel out of the parking lot.

Outside, the clouds turn gray and the wind picks up. Tiny drops of rain pelt my windshield as I idle at a red light. Thunder cracks. A bolt of lightning strikes the sign for Samantha's Thrift Store. I've learned from movies that whenever bolts of lightning strike anything, it means you should go there. The sky must know that I am lost and in need of direction. *But why Samantha's Thrift Store?* I need to get home before I attack any more salespeople. The light turns green. I lift my shaky foot off the brake pedal and drive into the parking lot.

I navigate through aisles of donated clothes, dirty household trinkets, and faulty electronics until I reach the used furniture section. Henry's E-Z-Rest sits in the center of the abandoned items. I sneak past three-legged chairs, drink-ringed coffee tables, and drawerless dressers until I am face-to-face with the long-lost bed-chair. The once puffy and smooth gray leather is pushed down from use and covered in stains. I'm surprised Samantha took it in. I check the price tag: $40. I can probably talk her down to twenty.

⊜ ⊜ ⊜

"Forty dollars," demands the cashier.

I open my wallet and hand the woman two twenties.

"All sales are final," she says as the cash register drawer shoots open. "Do you need help getting the recliner out of the store?"

"Ah . . . um . . ."

"Well?"

"Sure," I say. "Is that okay?"

She grabs the intercom phone that's mounted on the register light pole.

"ALAN UP FRONT FOR CUSTOMER ASSIS-TANCE. ALAN UP FRONT FOR CUSTOMER ASSIS-TANCE."

Some kid appears. "Hi," he says. "I'm Alan."

"Tom."

I explain how I bought the E-Z-Rest and need help securing it to my car.

"I'll grab the dolly and some rope," he says.

Twenty minutes later, the E-Z-Rest is tied to the roof of my LaPree.

"Thanks again," I say. "Sorry for taking up your time."

"It's cool," he says.

I don't know why he thinks it's cool. This must be his first job. Or maybe "it's cool" is code for "I hope you crash on the car ride home and die."

Tip of the Day: Removing a recliner from the roof of your car in the rain and then dragging it up three flights of stairs by yourself takes a very long time and causes sniffles, aggravation, and back problems.

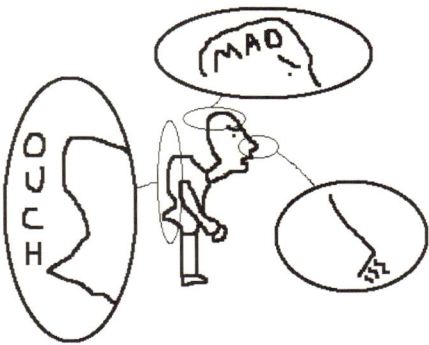

Once the E-Z-Rest is wiped down and placed back on top of the carpet circle, I face the TV and position myself with my back to the recliner. All I need to do is sit in the king's chair and I will become king. I will be popular. I will get Lisa. The E-Z-Rest has always been Henry's main power source. Once I sit down, I will absorb his strength and confidence and ability to communicate with others. Henry will become weak and insecure and once again, mute.

I bend my knees and let my body sink into the recliner. A strong force enters me. I pull the wooden handle and rest my arms on the cold armrests. THUNDER! WIND! RAIN! The apartment shakes. I aim the remote and press power. The TV slowly comes alive, and all sorts of black-and-white fuzz fills the screen. I turn up the volume so I can hear the crackling of the static. I want to know what it feels like to be Henry. I lean back on the E-Z-Rest and recline until I can't recline any further. I feel stuck. The TV crackles and pops. I sit/lie and watch the fuzzy screen. I don't need cable. I can make up my own TV show. This fuzz show is a show about people. Millions of fuzzy people fighting each other. The static's the noise they make, the chaos they bring on one another, on themselves. The constant bickering, the questions, the annoying racket—all static. Not one fuzzy is still or silent. No one takes time out to breathe or listen. Hate. War. Death. I turn up the volume. I want to hear the millions of fuzzy voices. *ME! ME! ME!* they shout. No sympathy. No silence. *Can you help ME? ME need some good dipping chips. Where's ME bathroom? Idiot! Asshole! Loser! TOM MITCHELL OUT FOR CARTS! TOM MITCHELL OUT FOR CARTS! She's beautiful. We'll always be friends. DIE!* My name's Mitchell. Tom Mitchell. I hate my name. It reminds me of some loser with some horrible skin disease. *I named you after my father.* Tom Mitchell one. Tom Mitchell two. Tom Mitchell three. *IDIOT! ASSHOLE! LOSER!* I turn up the volume. "Can you hear me?" I ask. "CAN YOU HEAR ME?!" I scream. The fuzzy voices continue crackling. Louder! And LOUDER! They engulf my words and steal my breath. No one listens. No one stops. People live and I die. I die over and over again. I sink deeper into the E-Z-Rest and melt away. Gone. Erased. Forgotten. The fuzzy voices live on.

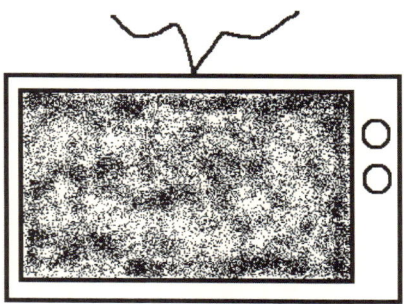

The apartment door opens. A dark figure walks inside and turns on the light.

"SURPRISE!" I yell.

Henry drops his *moving out for good* box and points at the E-Z-Rest. "What's that doing here?"

"It's always been here," I say.

"I got rid of it."

I push myself off the recliner and turn on the TV. "I ordered cable, too." Nothing but fuzz. "It's not activated yet, but this fuzzy show is pretty good."

Henry doesn't say anything.

"Have a seat," I tell him.

He doesn't move.

I walk over and grab his arm. "This way."

He shakes me loose.

"I'm not sitting on that thing."

"This is where you belong."

"Huh?"

"Just have a seat."

Henry grabs his *moving out for good* box and begins collecting his belongings.

"What are you doing?" I ask.

Nothing.

"*I said*, what are you doing?"

Nothing again.

I walk over to the recliner. "He's packing like he's leaving," I say to the E-Z-Rest. "He doesn't like us anymore."

"Who are you talking to?" Henry asks.

"I'm talking to my friend E-Z. Now please excuse us." I resume talking to the recliner. "Sure, we can ride our bikes up to Night Burger. You're so much better than that new Henry. The new Henry's a fake. He eats dumb healthy food and dresses like a stupid adult. I hate him. You know, he stole my girlfriend. What kind of best friend does that?"

"Enough!" Henry yells.

"I don't hear anything," I say to E-Z. "Do you?"

Henry storms up to me. "Do you have any idea how hard it was for me to get rid of that thing?"

"He's not my best friend anymore. You're my best friend." I wrap my arms around the recliner and give it a hug. "Oh yeah, once the cable is activated, we can watch TV all night long!"

Henry shoves me to the floor. "Fuck you!"

"Fuck me?!" I yell. "Fuck *you!*" I stand and punch the E-Z-Rest. "Fuck you!" Tears pour from my eyes as I punch the recliner again and again. "FUCK YOU!"

"I'm outta here." Henry abandons his *moving out for good* box and heads for the door. "You need some serious help, Tom."

I stop punching E-Z and look at Henry. "*I* need some serious help?! I wasn't the one who sat on a recliner for eight years watching TV!"

"You don't know anything about it."

"Oh, your dad died. Big deal. All dads die. Yours was a crook anyway. Normal guys don't blow up in cars!"

"Don't talk about my dad."

"He's DEAD!" I yell. "All you have left is that furry mom of yours!"

"SHUT UP!"

"I'm Henry, my mom and dad never loved each other, I want an E-Z-Rest, I'm a big, dumb, football player—"

Henry tackles me to the ground and starts choking me. *Kill me! Kill me!*

"I hate you!" Henry squeezes harder. "I HATE YOU!"

My head tingles. I feel light-headed. Henry's whole body shakes. I try to breathe but can't. I give up. Henry releases my throat. I cough and swallow giant gulps of air. Everything's blurry. The apartment door opens. Slams shut. I curl up into a ball and close my eyes.

twenty-two

"**H**ELLO," I said.

Henry looked up from his E-Z-Rest. "Hello . . . Tom."

He talked slower than I remembered. It was probably due to his weight gain and hair and beard growth.

"What are you watching?" I asked.

"Some movie about talking farm animals." He aimed the remote and muted the volume. "It's good but sad."

I scanned the living room. Nothing had really changed since the last time I was there. The only new addition was this furry brown blanket covering Henry's legs.

"That's new," I said, pointing to the blanket.

"My mom bought it for me. It's one hundred percent coyote."

"Nice." I sat on the couch. "So what's up?"

"Nothing," he said. "You?"

"Nothing."

We sat in silence. It was like we'd forgotten how to talk to one another. "Go on any bike rides lately?" I asked.

"No."

"Eat at Night Burger?"

"No."

"Play any football?"

"No."

"So for the past year and a half, you've been sitting on the E-Z-Rest watching TV?"

"Yeah," Henry snapped. "Something wrong with that?"

I didn't want to start an argument, so I changed the subject. "Anything new and exciting in the TV world?"

According to Henry, TV could be broken down into three main categories: daytime, afternoon, and evening.

"Think of it as breakfast, lunch, and dinner," he said.

"Got it."

He told me how watching all three categories played a vital role in maintaining a healthy TV diet. He also told me there was a secret category that not many people knew about.

"What's that?" I asked.

"Late-night TV," he replied. "Snack time."

I continued to sit on the couch as Henry talked on and on about his favorite channels, his daily TV schedule, and how, thanks to his lightning-fast remote skills, he once watched three shows simultaneously without missing any of the action.

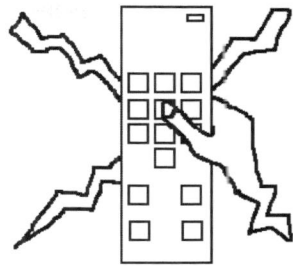

TV allowed Henry to escape his own world and enter a world of sitcoms, movies, music videos, and so on. Last Friday, he saved the universe by defeating a fire-breathing space monster. The Friday before that, he won over the hearts of millions by rescuing a little girl from drowning. I can't recall half the names of all the beautiful women he made love to on various shorelines. The passion he had for the square picture box reminded me of Cassie, and as he continued talking, my mind drifted off to old memories of her and I eating lunch, kissing, holding hands . . .

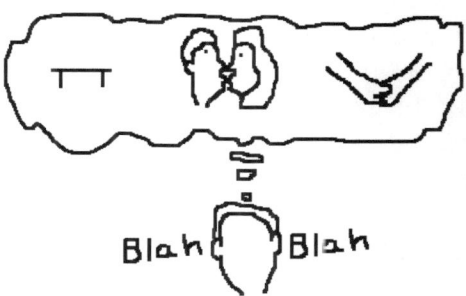

"And that will allow us to one day work through TVs," Henry explained. "Turning on the TV will be like clocking into the office."

I had no idea what he was talking about. "Interesting."

"Yep."

"Have you ever watched *Four Seasons?*" I asked.

"What channel's that on?"

"Two."

Henry started laughing. "No, no, no," he said. "I don't mess with basic TV."

"Why not?"

"Basic TV is simply a lower-class television service for lower-class people." He tossed out a bunch of statistics on how people who watch basic TV are dumber than cable watchers and rattled off all the amazing cable shows he was watching. *"Silent Sunday, High-Rise Decision, Ted's Travel Hour—"*

"Hold on," I said. *"Four Seasons* is a great show."

"Nothing produced on basic TV is a great show."

"Trust me, it's good."

"No way, shows on basic TV are stupid."

"Well, I think your cable shows are stupid."

"First off, you've never seen most of my shows because you don't have cable, and second, you can't argue with a guy who knows everything about TV."

"You don't know everything about TV," I said.

"I think I do," Henry replied.

"You don't!"

"I do!"

"Just because you sit on that stupid recliner and watch TV all day doesn't make you an expert."

"This recliner is not stupid!" Henry shouted.

"Ever since you got it, you haven't done anything but sit around and watch TV."

"So? What should I be doing? Taking classes at Token like you?"

"Yeah."

"Look." Henry aimed the remote at me. "I don't tell you how to live your life, so don't tell me how to live mine."

"I'm only trying to help," I said. "You can't sit on that thing forever. Eventually you'll have to get a job or something."

"Didn't you hear what I said earlier?" Henry asked. "In a few years, people will be working from the TV."

"Doing what?"

Henry threw up his arms and smacked them down on the recliner armrests. "Any sort of job imaginable."

"That doesn't make sense," I said. "What if the job's a garbage man? You can't be a garbage man by sitting in front of a TV."

"Weren't you listening when I explained how it all worked?"

"Yeah," I said.

"Doesn't sound like it," Henry replied. "Good thing you're going to college."

"What does that mean?"

"Your listening skills are terrible."

"I'm not taking listening classes."

"You should."

"Okay." I got up off the couch. "I didn't come here for this."

"Wait." Henry collapsed the leg rest and transformed the bed-chair into a chair.

"What?" I asked.

"I'm sorry." He lowered his head. "Don't leave."

Henry talked about how losing his dad in the car explosion made him depressed and confused. "I only feel normal when sitting on this E-Z-Rest," he said. "I think it's because it was my last memory of him alive."

I sat on the couch not knowing what to say.

"You want to hear something crazy?" he whispered.

"Sure."

"I think my mom's happy that he's gone."

"Why do you think that?" I asked.

Henry held up his coyote blanket. "Fur."

"What?"

"Remember all those fur coat fights my mom and dad would get into?"

"Yeah."

"Well, the first thing my mom did after the funeral was buy a fur scarf. Then she bought me this coyote blanket. You should see her bedroom. Fur everywhere."

I wasn't a detective, but the situation (Henry's dad hating fur, his mom loving fur, then Henry's dad going kaboom, and now Henry's mom buying fur) seemed a bit fishy. I wasn't about to accuse Henry's mom of murder, though, so I blurted out, "I had a girlfriend."

Henry readjusted himself on the recliner. "You had a girlfriend?"

"Her name was Cassie."

"When did this happen?"

"I met her at community college," I said. "She walked up to me while I was eating lunch and made me try a piece of her peanut butter and jelly sandwich."

"You hate peanut butter and jelly."

"I know." I continued the story. "We ate lunch together, became best friends, talked on the phone, rode bikes, Night Burger, summer, fireworks, lake house, boats, love, sex—"

"You had sex," interrupted Henry.

"Yeah," I said. "A few times. It was good, but it ended up destroying the relationship."

"How so?"

"You know, after the sex, she wanted the ring and kids and house. I wasn't ready for that."

"Who broke up with who?" Henry asked.

"I'm not sure, but we got into this big argument over aliens and stopped talking to one another."

"You haven't talked to her since?"

"No," I said. "She got a restraining order against me so I ended up dropping out of school."

"So you're not going to community college anymore?"

"Nope."

"Wow," Henry said. "I knew college was uncomfortable, but that's ridiculous."

The talking farm animal show still played on the muted television. A pig priest was speaking next to a tiny casket surrounded by goats, cows, ducks, horses, and chickens. I couldn't hear what was being said, but several of the mourning animals held signs that read: *DEATH TO ALL HUMANS!*

"I was thinking," Henry said. "Would you be interested in getting an apartment together?"

"YES!" I yelled. "But . . . I don't have much money saved up."

"That's all right. My mom sold the used car lot after my dad died and got a bunch of money."

The case of the fur-addicted murdering wife thickens.

"So you're rich?" I asked.

"Pretty much," he said. "My dad didn't have a will, so all the money went to my mom. She buys me anything I want, though."

"Wow," I said. "That's awesome."

"I guess."

"So when do you plan on moving?" I asked.

"As soon as possible."

I picked up Henry the next morning around 10 a.m.

"This is exciting," I said.

"Yeah," he replied as he got into my LaPree.

His eyes were barely open. I'm sure he was up all night snacking a.k.a. watching late-night TV.

"What time did you go to bed last night?"

"Why?"

"You look like you're about to fall asleep."

"I'll be fine."

As we drove, Henry kept squirming around in the car seat.

"Why do you keep moving around like that?" I asked.

"I can't get comfortable."

"That's probably from sitting on that E-Z-Rest for so long," I said. "You can't get comfortable in any other seat."

We pulled into the Glenshire Square strip mall parking lot and exited my LaPree. I originally wanted to ride bikes to the real estate office, but Henry didn't think we'd be taken seriously.

"If you worked at a real estate place and two guys came riding up on bikes, would you rent them an apartment?"

"Probably not," I said.

"Exactly."

The entire process, from the moment we entered Tent Real Estate until we signed an actual lease, took almost ten hours. Most of the time was spent driving around with our leasing agent and looking at various places. Once we found a place we both liked and Henry pulled out his checkbook, things moved pretty quickly.

"Is the apartment in Glenshire?" asked my fake dad.

"No," I said as I set down my fork. "Dire."

"Why Dire?" asked my fake mom. "There's nothing out there."

"We want to be away from everything."

"How many rooms?" asked my fake dad.

"One bedroom, one bathroom."

"Who gets the bedroom?" asked my fake mom.

"Me," I said. "Henry wants to sleep in the living room."

My fake dad raised his drinking glass. "Congratulations, Tom."

We all clinked glasses.

"Just promise me one thing," said my fake mom.

"What's that?" I asked.

"Don't ever come back."

Henry and I spent the weekend packing and moving into our new apartment. The hardest thing to move was definitely the E-Z-Rest. We ended up tying it to the top of my LaPree with some rope. Henry made me promise not to drive over 30 miles per hour and suggested I put my flashers on. Some drivers must not have liked how slow I was traveling because they sped past, honking and screaming obscenities out their windows.

⊜ ⊜ ⊜

"You hungry?" I asked Henry after everything was moved in.

"Yeah," he replied. "Can you go grocery shopping?"

"I don't have much experience."

"There's nothing to it."

"You want to come with?" I asked.

"Can't." He plopped himself on the recliner. "I have to wait here for the cable guy."

⊜ ⊜ ⊜

I drove over to Vick's Produce and bought a bunch of stuff while Henry hung back.

"What is this crap?" he asked as he helped unpack the groceries. "Popcorn. Chips."

"What?"

"You shouldn't buy popcorn that's named Popcorn, or chips named Chips."

"Why not?" I asked. "It's cheaper."

"Generic food tastes like crap."

"Well, I don't have much money."

"That's fine," Henry said. "I'll buy the groceries from now on."

"I don't see what's so bad about this food." I opened a bag of Cookies and ate one. "These cookies taste good."

The apartment intercom buzzed.

"Cable guy," Henry said as he walked toward the intercom. "Think of it this way. Name-brand food is like cable TV, and generic food is like basic TV. Understand?"

I nodded.

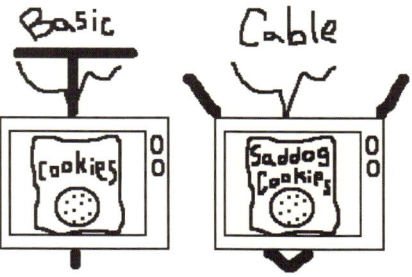

Our first night as roommates was spent in the living room watching cable TV. Henry felt bad that I had nowhere to sit and told me he would order a couch from Forever Furniture on Monday.

"You sure?" I said.

"Yeah, no problem."

The movie we were watching was called *Dent*. It was about this customer who goes crazy after his car gets dented by a shopping cart.

"He's going to kill the employees?" I asked.

"Yeah," Henry said. "He's pissed."

"How does he know it's the employees' fault? For all he knows, some customer could have caused the damage."

POP! POP! POP!

"Too late now," Henry said.

Living with Henry was great; however, we formed this weird habit of saying *hello* whenever we ran into one another. We were never like that growing up, but once we became roommates, we were greeting each other constantly. In the kitchen, living room, bathroom—*hello, hello, hello.* The hellos were getting out of hand.

KNOCK! KNOCK! KNOCK!

"Come in."

My bedroom door opened and Henry entered. "Hello, Tom."

"Hello, Henry."

"Can we talk?"

"Sure." I rolled off my air mattress and followed him into the living room. "What's up?"

Henry sat on his E-Z-Rest and reclined. "I can't take these hellos anymore."

I sat on the blue couch. "I know what you mean."

"It seems pointless to say *hello* when you live with someone."

"Exactly."

Henry sat upright on his E-Z-Rest, held out his hand as if to make a pact. "No more hellos."

I shook his hand and repeated, "No more hellos."

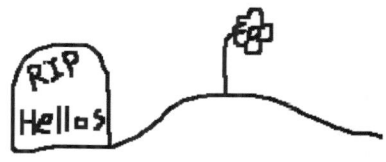

Over the next however many months, my life and Henry's life merged into one. The living room became our sanctuary, the square picture box our God. We worshipped cable TV for providing us with a healthy serving of shows at all hours of the day and night. Dark bags formed under our eyes. Hair grew in odd places. Bones ached. Eventually life took the form of death as we lost the strength to move from our habitual positions, I on the blue couch and Henry on the E-Z-Rest.

⊜ ⊜ ⊜

"We . . . go on . . . bike ride," I suggested one exceptionally frail morning.

Henry slowly turned to me and snarled, "I . . . watch."

"All . . . we do," I slurred, "is watch."

"*Quiet!*"

"What's . . . your problem?" I asked.

"NOTHING!" he rasped. "Go . . . to your room!"

"You're not . . . my parents."

"I pay . . . cable bill."

I dragged myself off the couch and stumbled to my bedroom.

"And I pay . . . gas bill!" Henry bellowed. "And electric! And food!"

I slammed my bedroom door shut and collapsed on my air mattress. I couldn't live like this any longer. I needed to stop depending on Henry. I needed to escape the apartment. I needed a job.

twenty-three

I STAB THE E-Z-REST with the big kitchen knife. "Die, Henry!" I say. "DIE!"

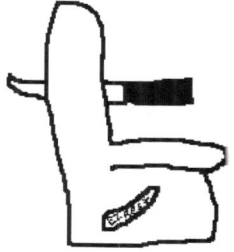

  I leave the apartment and drive to Rudy's. My neck is still all red from Henry trying to murder me last night. I should report him to the police but can't. I'm pretty much the most wanted criminal around. Toilet paper theft. Salesman assault. Murderous thoughts. I can't walk into the station and be like, "Hello, I want to report a crime." The cops would pull out their guns and blow me away. *POP! POP! POP!* Dead. That's the problem with being a criminal. If something bad happens to me (like my ex-best friend trying to murder me), I'm forced to take justice into my own hands. I never thought I'd grow up to be an outlaw, but I don't think anyone grows up to be exactly what they imagined they would. *Beep. Beep. Beep.* There are those beeps again. I've been hearing them inside my head for about three months now. I haven't mentioned it because people who hear noises are typically crazy. I'm not crazy. Someone's probably recording my thoughts. It's either that or someone's controlling my thoughts. I could have been abducted recently. I might not even be human. Maybe I'm just some test subject sent down by the aliens.

The Rudy's parking lot is packed with cars and people; there's even a big gray elephant. I give up my search for an open space and park across the street in the Toy Universe lot. I wish they were the ones having the grand re-opening. I hate how customers get so excited over free samples, discounted prices, and balloons for the kids. If my life ever gets to the point where I'm getting excited over grand re-openings, I'm driving my car off a cliff. That's a cool way to die.

I stand near the edge of Davis Street and contemplate running into oncoming traffic. Too bad splattering my body against someone's car goes against my No-Bother Policy. The driver would have to get a car wash, deal with the insurance company, and fill out a police report.

"My whole day's ruined because of you!" I imagine the driver screaming at my bloody body

I don't respond because I'm dead.

"Don't act like you can't hear me!" yells the angry driver.

I think getting into arguments with dead people is fine. Some people can only talk to the dead because they're afraid to say what they want to the living. I never talked much to my fake parents when they were alive. I thought I'd talk to them more once they were dead, but that's not the case.

As soon as the traffic clears, I hurry across the street and enter the Rudy's parking lot. "Excuse me," I say as I push my way through the crowd. "Excuse me."

A hairy, bug-eyed customer grabs me. "Wait your turn," he scolds.

Part of me wants to unzip my sweatshirt and show him my Rudy's uniform, but the fear of what would happen if I exposed my employee identity keeps me quiet.

I follow the crowd as we slowly approach the entrance doors. Once up front, I freeze. The big orange letters that once spelled Rudy's are no more. I no longer work at *Rudy's*. I now work at *Henry's*.

The inside is crammed with customers. Music plays over the intercom. *Da da de-de da da de.* Pete must have finally fixed the store radio. *Grand Re-opening* signs hang from the ceiling. Balloons. Confetti. Free samples. Two-for-ones. Twenty-five percent offs. "Mitchell!" Pete stands on top of the customer service counter holding a megaphone.

"CARTS!" his voice booms. "NOW!"

"I haven't clocked in yet!" I shout.

"No time!"

I try to walk but can't. There are too many customers. Their echoing voices and powerful bodies trap me. Cover me. Drown me. " !" I scream. " !" No one hears me. *Beep. Beep. Beep.* Everything goes black. *Aslfkj sdlfkjdsf asldfkjl.* My thoughts make no sense. This is the end. Death by the unforgiving Sea of Customers. Someone suddenly grabs my arm and rescues me. My eyes reactivate. It's Pat Markowitz from the Women's Circle. She tosses me into the cereal aisle. "What's going on?" My voice returns. More women appear. They barricade the end of the aisle. I turn. The Old Men barricade the other end. Cereal boxes fall to the floor as the Voyeurs crawl out from the shelves. Gary falls from the ceiling. Raven soars in. Stan cruises up on a motorized cart. The three form a small triangle around me. I stand in the center. There's no escape.

"Time's up," whispers Gary.

"Join us," says Raven.

Stan smiles. "Hop on, Tom."

I always wished this day would never come. I have to think. I have to join a side.

"Face it," states Gary. "You're one of us."

"Don't listen to him!" snaps Raven. "He doesn't even know your real age!"

Gary hisses at her.

"There are no customers in the back room," says Stan. "Just friendly faces and good old-fashioned conversation."

The three move in closer. I can see Stan's neck mole, smell Raven's hair spray, and hear Gary's tight red pants stretching at the seams. They start chanting "Choose!

Choose! Choose!" Their bodies tower over me (except Stan's because he's on that motorized cart). The overhead fluorescent lights dim. I sink into the tile floor. "Choose! Choose! Choose!" Darker. Darker. The last bit of light disappears. *Da da de-de*— The music cuts out. This is the end of Tom Mitchell. They want to create something new—a person who will fight for their cause, think how they think, do what they do. No more on my own. No more hiding. No more outlaw lifestyle. "CHOOSE! CHOOSE! CHOOSE!" I sink deeper into the floor and absorb their words. They're killing me. I can't move. Can't think. Can't anything. I want to be at Henry's house. I want to be riding bikes. I want to be eating at Night Burger. I don't want this life. It's no good. Nothing will ever be as good as it used to be. Everything's changed—my fake parents are dead, my best friend hates me, my whole life has turned into war. I'm sick of it. "CHOOSE! CHOOSE! CHOOSE!" Their chants continue but are now muffled by my thoughts, my anger, my *being* rushing to the surface. *I DON'T CARE!* I'm tired of hiding who I am. I'm tired of this job. I'm tired of living this fake adult life. *Hello. Have a great day. I apologize for the inconvenience.* It's a lie. The entire system is a lie. I can't take it. "CHOOSE! CHOOSE! CHOOSE!" No more fear. No more silence. No more groups. They don't know what's best for me. They only want me to give up my power so they can become stronger. *NO!* I'm not giving in. Nothing exists to me anymore. Not friends. Not family. Not Rudy's (I mean, Henry's). Not even myself. I'm pushing through and entering new terrain. I'm challenging the source of everything that exists. I've been lost in a world of confusion, lies, and hate that was constructed from years of dealing with annoying customers and never saying what I wanted. The pot of boiling water has finally bubbled over and no lid can suppress my heated emotions. I feel an urge to live but drift into some dead consciousness that I cannot explain. Time moves and all I see are thousands of winged clocks with their hands spinning wildly out of control. My black-and-white world is painted over, creating a new world full of colors derived from all my feelings that I kept inside. I am no longer in human form. Something more? Or perhaps something less? *Go tell everyone I'm an employee voyeur. Go tell everyone I hate customers. Go tell everyone all my fears and insecurities! Tell everyone everything!*

I rise up. "STOP!"

Gary, Raven, and Stan step (or, in Stan's case, reverse) back. The overhead fluorescents burn my eyes. I lift my hands to shield the light. "I'm not joining any group!"

The three stare at me.

"I'm not fighting in your war." I put my hands down. "So do whatever it is you all have to do. Say what you have to say. Ruin me. Kill me. I don't care anymore."

Gary, Raven, and Stan stand (or, in Stan's case, sit) in silence.

"But—"

"NO!" I shout.

Gary grabs my arm. "This is your destiny!"

"Get your cum hands off me!"

I break through the triangle and leave.

"Tom, wait!" Raven yells.

"Walter's going to be very disappointed," says Stan.

"*Get back here!*" Gary screams. "*This is war!*"

I corral the last row of carts and reenter Henry's. Everything's quiet. No music plays. No cash registers beep. No one's talking or moving or anything. It feels like everyone's staring at me. I walk down the canned food aisle and head to the break room. Customers stand frozen—reading sales papers, pushing shopping carts, and holding grocery items.

"You have no right to hate us!" someone yells.

I reach the break room and open the door. A group of women stands dressed in body armor and armed with guns, grenades, and rocket launchers. I immediately close the door and turn around. Lisa. She slaps me across the face. "You fucking cereal box pervert!"

Customers start to unfreeze. "Attack! Kill!" they shout.

I run into the fruit and vegetable section. Apples, oranges, potatoes, onions, pears, and all sorts of fruits and veggies rain down on me. I shield my head with my hands and take cover in the center divider aisle. A giant old man stands before me: Walter.

"You need to learn how to respect your elders," he says.

I sprint for the juice aisle but he blocks it with his enormous Velcro shoe.

"ATTENTION, HENRY'S SHOPPERS. TOM MITCHELL IS IN THE CENTER DIVIDER AISLE. REPEAT. TOM MITCHELL IS IN THE CENTER DIVIDER AISLE. PLEASE KILL HIM."

Walter breathes in deep and blows out. I'm knocked to the ground. The sole of his giant Velcro shoe towers over me. I roll away just as it crashes onto the grocery floor. *BOOM!* The entire store shakes. Lights flicker. Items fall off the shelves. I get to my feet and cut down the bread aisle. Gary and his crew of voyeurs crawl out of the shelves and fall from the ceiling. I turn around. Two eggs pelt me in the eyes. I wipe away bits of shell and slimy yolk and run blindly toward the Voyeurs. "Ahhh!" One of them grabs my sweatshirt. It's Cory the Cork.

"Let go!" I yell.

We struggle. A small remote falls out of his pocket. I pick it up and press *Turbo*. He screams in painful ecstasy and releases me. Another Voyeur grabs my sweatshirt hood. I'm choking.

"Hold him, boys!" announces Gary.

I unzip my sweatshirt and break for the entrance. It's blocked off by the High School and College Kids. "Weirdo! Loser! Creep!" they scream.

POP! POP! POP!

Two-liter bottles of pop explode on the endcap in front of me. I dive onto the tile floor. The Women's Circle is moving in. *CRASH!* Glass shatters as customers chanting "We're always right! We're always right!" burst through the storefront windows.

I stand and run for Pete's office. Shopping carts come at me from all directions. I move from side to side to avoid them. A shell from a rocket launcher hits an endcap full of

Bergen's Chili. The blast sends cans flying everywhere. One can hits me in the head. *THUNK!* I'm knocked to the floor. Pop cans, salad dressing bottles, and milk gallons pelt my body. "Ow! Ow! Ow!" The hairy, bug-eyed customer who scolded me outside earlier climbs to the top shelf, yells "FREEDOM!" and jumps on top of me.

"I GOT HIM!" he screams. "HE'S OURS!"

I lift my head and see a wall of angry customers and employees closing in.

"HURRY!" the man screams. *"HURRY!"*

I stretch for one of the chili cans but can't quite reach it. *"KILL! KILL!"* GIANT OLD MAN STEP! GIANT OLD MAN STEP! *"KILL! KILL!"* I stretch further. Further! I tap the can with my middle finger. *Almost.* I tap it again. *Got it!* I bash the can of chili over the customer's head. Blood gushes as he rolls off me. I get to my feet and sprint for Pete's office.

"OPEN UP!" I scream as I pound on the door with both fists. "OPEN UP!"

The office door bursts open.

"Get in here, Mitchell!" Pete pulls me inside and slams the door shut. *BANG! BANG! BANG!* He wipes his sweaty forehead with his black-and-white polka-dot handkerchief.

"Jesus, Mitchell!" he says. "You started a war out there!"

"I started a war?!"

BANG! BANG! BANG!

"You couldn't choose a side! You had to be different!"

"Different?!" I scream. "I just didn't want to fight in *their* war!"

"THEIR war?!" Pete gives me a weird look. "This is *YOUR* war!"

"What are you talking about?"

Pete grabs my shirt and pulls me toward the door. "NO, PLEASE!" I beg. "DON'T OPEN IT!"

He turns the silver handle. "This is what YOU created!"

The office door flies open, revealing a world of flames and death. Customers and employees scream and fight and kill one another. Bodies chopped in half by frozen pizzas. Brains melted by register scanners. Hearts exploding from excessive red meat consumption. Blood! Blood everywhere! Gary, Raven, and Walter stand together laughing amid complete chaos. Henry sits on an E-Z-Rest throne. Lisa sits next to him. Surrounding them are the High School and College Kids. "All hail the king and queen!" they chant. "All hail the king and queen!" Everything suddenly turns upside down and starts spinning. Round and round. Faster and faster. Pete slams the door shut.

"You *see?!*" he shouts.

"But the Old Men and the Women's Circle and the Voyeurs," I say. "They were the ones at war."

"You were at war with them!" Pete yells.

LOUD BANG!

"I had high hopes for ya, Mitchell." Pete walks up to me. "I need that shirt and name tag."

I hesitate.

LOUD BANG! LOUD BANG!

"NOW!"

I unpin my name tag and remove my Rudy's shirt.

"You're lucky I'm not calling the cops," he says. "Ya know what they do to toilet paper thieves in the big house?"

I don't say anything.

"Didn't think I knew about that, did ya?" he says. "Let me tell ya something. We know all about ya now, Mitchell. The whole stinking world does."

LOUD BANG! LOUD BANG! LOUD BANG!

The office door starts to bend. Pete opens the bottom desk drawer and hands me a flashlight. "Here."

"What am I supposed to do with this?"

"Escape!"

DOOR BENDING BANG! DOOR BENDING BANG!

Pete reaches underneath his office desk and pushes a button. One of the ceiling tiles opens up and a ladder comes down.

"Go on," he says.

DOOR BENDING BANG! DOOR BENDING BANG!

I stick the flashlight in my pocket and climb the ladder.

"Follow the yellow beam till you reach the end," Pete tells me. "You'll find a rope tied to it. Use that to climb to safety."

"Why are you helping me?" I ask.

Pete grabs a bag of Zolo's Chips off his desk. "I envy ya, Mitchell."

BOOM!

The office door bursts open. Customers and employees rush inside. Pete and his chips go flying.

I click on the flashlight and hurry across the yellow beam. I find the rope. *CLANK!* I shine the light into the darkness. Gary. "You'll never escape us!" I kick out the ceiling tile, grab the rope, and climb down. The grocery floor looks like a battlefield. Dead bodies. Destroyed aisles. Abandoned shopping carts. Dismembered poultry. "He's trying to ESCAPE!!!" shouts Gary.

I release the rope and bolt out of Henry's. Everyone's chasing me. "MOUSE! MOUSE! MOUSE!" I scream as I run across the parking lot. The elephant moans and goes wild. Cars smash. People scatter. I run onto Davis Street. Tires screech. Metal collides. I trip. The angry crowd closes in. Walter mounts the elephant. Henry's Grocery is one giant red flame. *BEEP! BEEP! BEEP!* "Get the hell off the road!" I stand and run across the Toy Universe lot. Keys. Unlock door. Inside. Door lock! Door lock! Door lock! Hands shaking. Drop keys. "CRAP!" Customers and employees pile onto my car. *THUD! THUD! THUD!* The windshield cracks. Keys. Ignition. Turn. The engine revs. I shift into drive and floor it. Can't see. Turn on wipers. Bodies crash to the pavement. "THERE!" *An opening. An escape!* I press the gas pedal to the floor and fly onto Davis Street. Passing cars. Blowing stoplights. One, two, three hundred miles per hour. Everyone in my rearview mirror gets smaller and smaller until they eventually disappear.

twenty-four

"**I** THINK I'm finished," I said.

Pete set his bag of Zolo's Chips on the office desk.

"One sec." He licked his red-powdered fingers clean and wiped them dry on his black pants. "Let's see."

I handed him the employment forms. He leaned back on his fancy desk chair and reviewed the pages.

"Good . . . good . . ."

The office was small and plain-looking. There was a desk, two chairs, some file cabinets, a big safe, surveillance TV, and a bunch of framed certificates hanging on the white walls.

". . . good . . . good . . . all set." Pete rolled his chair toward the gray filing cabinet. "I'm also gonna need to take your fingerprints."

"Really?" I asked.

"Relax," Pete said as he opened one of the file drawers. "I'm only joking with ya, Mitchell."

Pete was the afternoon shift manager at Rudy's Grocery. He looked like a big, balding tomato with glasses. I didn't tell him that. I didn't tell him anything that I was actually thinking. I lied a lot during the interview process.

"Do you like customer service?"

"Yes."

"Do you work well in a team setting?"

"Yes."

"Do you like to follow the rules?"

"Yes."

If I didn't lie, I don't think Pete would have hired me. I wasn't about to go back out on the streets searching for jobs. I applied all over Cary—Good Smells Lumber, Fill It Up Gas, Budget Crafts. Rudy's was the first place to call me back. I was ready to tell Pete whatever he wanted to hear. He could have asked me to marry him and I would have said yes. That was how much I hated looking for jobs. The whole process of entering random businesses and asking for an application made me uncomfortable. I tried dragging Henry along with me, but he had no interest in the job search. All he wanted to do was sit on his E-Z-Rest and watch TV. He was lucky his dad blew up in that car.

"What size shirt?" Pete asked as he closed the file drawer.

"Medium," I said.

He rolled his chair toward a clear plastic bin, popped off the lid, and pulled out a red collared shirt.

"Take care of this," he said as he gently handed it to me. "This is your baby."

I rolled the shirt into a ball and set it on my lap.

"Listen up!" Pete snapped the lid back on the plastic bin and rolled himself back toward his desk. "Rudy's uniform policy: that shirt, tucked into khakis. Solid black gym shoes."

At Night Burger, we were given the shirt, pants, and hat. We were also allowed to wear whatever color shoes we wanted.

"I'll have a name tag for you tomorrow."

I nodded.

"Any questions?" Pete asked.

"No."

"Good." He smacked his thighs and stood up. I stood up too. "Be here tomorrow at two thirty. I wanna run over some ground rules, show ya how to clock in, fun stuff like that."

"All right."

"My gut's telling me good things about you, Mitchell." Pete grabbed his bag of Zolo's Chips and held it toward me. "Chip?"

"No thanks."

Pete shrugged and shoved a handful of dusty red chips into his mouth. "This job is onna hange your life," he mumbled.

Henry was sitting on the E-Z-Rest watching TV when I entered the apartment. He was wearing his TV clothes: navy jersey shorts and a white T-shirt.

"I got a job," I said.

"Where at?" Henry asked.

I threw my red Rudy's shirt on the blue couch and sat down. "This grocery store called Rudy's."

"Where's that?"

"Out in Cary."

"Why are you working all the way out in Cary?"

"Ah . . . they pay more out there."

"How much?"

"Eight an hour."

"Nice."

I could have told Henry the truth about why I was working so far away, but he never worked a day in his life and didn't understand how embarrassing it is when someone you recognize (even if you never spoke to them, which oftentimes makes it worse as they are probably thinking to themselves *I knew something was wrong with that guy*) walks into the place you work. I wouldn't care as much if I were a businessman or alien scientist, but I was a stocker at a grocery store.

"What are you watching?" I asked.

"Crap!" Henry aimed the remote at the TV and changed stations. "Nothing but crap on!"

There was something seriously wrong with Henry. He wasn't right in the head. His moods changed constantly. Some days he screamed. Some days he wouldn't talk. And some days he acted perfectly normal.

"My first day is tomorrow."

"CRAP!" Henry yelled.

"I'm going to be working the afternoon shift from three to eleven."

"AAAHHH!!!"

"Days off, Monday and Friday."

This was one of the tactics I used for calming him down. I had all sorts of tactics that allowed me to control his mind and get him to act just how I wanted. The tactic I was currently using was called Don't Acknowledge. Basically, if I didn't acknowledge his aggressive attitude, it wouldn't exist.

Henry stopped flipping stations. "Good luck with everything," he said.

"Thanks."

We spent the rest of the night sitting peacefully in the living room watching TV.

≋ ≋ ≋

"This bad boy over here is my Manager Training School certificate."

I sat in the Rudy's office while Pete talked on and on about all his different wall certificates.

"Merit High School Treasurer certificate. Woodworking certificate. This here is my lifeguard certificate. Betcha didn't think I could swim, huh?"

It didn't make sense why Pete made me show up thirty minutes early for this. I wouldn't care if I were getting paid, but I wasn't even clocked in. I wanted to ask Pete if we could start the training but didn't want to change the subject. When you're a kid, you can change the subject whenever you want, but not when you're an adult. I had to sit there and act interested in those stupid framed pieces of paper. If I said anything unrelated to the certificates, Pete would think I was uninterested, which would make him upset, and the last thing I wanted to do was make the manager upset on my first day.

"What about you, Mitchell?" Pete eventually asked. "You got any certificates?"

"No," I said.

"Keep working hard and maybe you'll get one some-day." Pete glanced at his watch. "Dang, 3:20 already. Let's get ya clocked in."

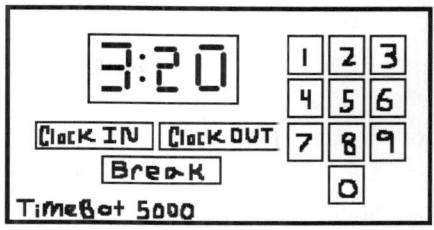

The time clock was mounted directly outside the office. My employee code was the last four digits of my Human Identification Number. I entered the digits on the electronic PIN pad and pushed the Clock In button.

"To clock out, enter your code and push Clock Out," Pete said. "For lunch, enter code and push Break. Listen up. When ya return from lunch, enter your code again and push Break again. Got it?"

"Yes."

"Good."

We reentered the office.

"I'm gonna have Ryan train you." He picked up the phone and made an announcement over the speakers.

"RYAN TO THE OFFICE. RYAN TO THE OFFICE."

About five minutes later, this skinny, shaggy-haired kid showed up.

"'Sup? I'm Ryan." He smacked me on the shoulder.

"Tom."

The kid looked like he was still in high school.

"Ryan's one of our all-star employees," Pete said. "Listen closely to what he has to say."

We opened the door to leave.

"Oh, almost forgot." Pete handed me a small piece of plastic. "Your name tag."

Ryan and I walked up and down the various aisles. "You'll be doing stock, recovery, carts, and other crap like that. You ever stock?"

"Kind of," I said.

He rolled his eyes. "It's just fucking grabbing whatever you're stocking and tossing it on the shelf."

He talked really fast, and whenever I asked him a question, he sighed really loud before answering.

"What is recovery again?" I asked.

LOUD SIGH. "Dude, I already told you, it's just fucking walking around the store and making shit look nice."

Getting trained by a teenager was the worst. He treated me like I was an idiot and spent the majority of time talking about how he was always getting his dick sucked.

"Alison sucks it on Mondays. Rachel on Tuesdays. Cindy's my weekend dick-sucker."

At the end of the training session, he gave me a quiz. Whenever I answered something incorrectly he shouted "WRONG!" and went over the correct answer like part of my brain was missing. "Okay, to get your stock, you walk to the back room, which is in the *back* of the store. You know what a *store* is, right?"

Ryan must have told everyone at Rudy's under the age of twenty-two that I was a loser or something, because no one in the high school or college age range wanted anything to do with me. The only people I consistently interacted with were Pete and the customers. There was also some woman employee with black hair named Raven, who asked me questions every so often. Stan was another employee I sort of knew just because I saw him whenever I went to the back room to take out the trash or get my stock. The only other employee I had any sort of contact with was this short guy named Gary who wore tight red pants and was always popping out of nowhere and saying hello to me.

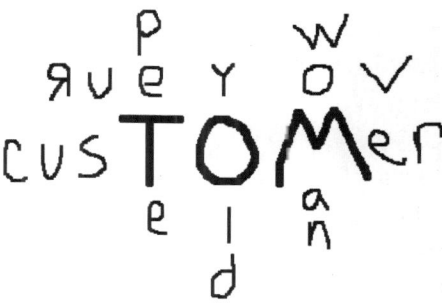

The customers at Rudy's were no different than those at Night Burger. All they did was complain and ask stupid questions. One time, when I was stocking some Red Barrel Oatmeal, this customer ran up to me and insisted I go to the salad dressing aisle with him. When I asked what the problem was, he shouted, "It's an emergency!"

"You see this junk?" He pulled me toward the shelf. "Falcon's Dressing."
"Yes."
"It's disgusting," he said. "*Yuck!*"
I told him that I had never tried Falcon's Dressing, so I wasn't sure how it tasted.

"You should know what it tastes like," he stated. "You work here."

"I just started three weeks ago."

"Typical excuse."

He explained how he had a coupon for the brand and decided to give it a try. "I usually don't mess with coupons, but the deal was too good to pass up. That's how they get you," he said. "They make you an offer you can't refuse."

After listening to him complain on and on about the disgusting taste and lumpy texture, he told me that he wanted me to remove the dressing from the shelf.

"I don't think I can do that."

"Sure you can."

"I only stock the items," I said. "I'm not authorized to remove them."

He called me a *liar* and yelled, "I want that Falcon's Dressing off the shelf NOW!"

When I told him I would get the manager, he opened one of the salad dressing bottles and poured the contents onto the tile floor.

"What are you doing?" I asked.

"God's work," he replied.

I ran to grab Pete.

When we returned to the aisle, the customer was gone and there was red salad dressing all over the floor. It looked like someone had been murdered. Pete approached the scene with extreme caution.

"We gotta tape this off pronto," he said. "Grab two carts from up front and get some CAUTION tape from Stan."

I stood there a second.

"Hurry!"

I got the carts and the tape and rushed back to the scene. Pete was down on his knees examining the mess.

"I got everything," I said.

Pete stood up. "Let's set up a perimeter."

We positioned the carts and wrapped the CAUTION tape around them.

"I'm gonna have to make a special cleanup call," Pete said. "Wait here till assistance arrives. Afterward, stop by my office so I can get your statement."

Pete opened the office door.

"Have a seat," he said.

I walked inside and sat down on the metal folding chair. Pete pulled out a small notebook and pen from his back pocket and started in with the questioning.

"What exactly happened in the salad dressing aisle, Mitchell?"

I explained how the customer was unsatisfied with the taste of the dressing and how he only bought it because he had this amazing coupon and how he wanted me to remove the dressing from the shelf, but I had told him that I was a stocker and removing items wasn't in my job description.

Pete flipped the notebook closed and stuck the pen behind his ear. "Ya told the customer *what?*"

"I told him I wasn't authorized to remove items."

"Look, Mitchell, next time, just do what the customer wants."

"So if a customer wants me to remove items from the shelf, I'm supposed to do it?"

"Exactly."

"What do I do with the items?"

"Just toss everything in a cart, and when the customer leaves, you can put it back."

"I don't understand the point of taking all the dressing off the shelf and then putting it back," I said. "It's a lot of extra work."

Pete sat on his fancy chair and grabbed his bag of Zolo's Chips. "Do you know anything about customer service?"

"Yes."

"I don't think you do."

According to Pete, customer service originated during the prehistoric period. He told me this story about a caveman store owner and how a caveman customer beat him to death. "It all started over a price disagreement," Pete said. "The customer claimed the owner's bone tool prices were too high, and the owner claimed the customer was being unreasonable. When the store owner told the customer to leave his store, the customer picked up a rock and split the store owner's skull open. Supposedly there was a cave trial and the caveman judge sided with the caveman customer, saying 'Og, og, employers must understand that in the business world, the customer is always right, og, og.'"

"That doesn't make any sense," I said.

"Well," Pete replied, "you're gonna have to make it make sense."

"So I have to do whatever the customer wants?"

"Exactly."

"What if they want something for a lower price?"

"Ya give 'em a lower price."

"What if they want to taste the food before buying it?"

"Ya let 'em taste the food."

"What if they want a back massage?"

"Then ya give 'em a freaking back massage!"

I sat in the metal folding chair not knowing what to say.

"Look, Mitchell," Pete said as he shoved his mouth full of chips. "Just be hankful ou're not etting your skull cracked open."

twenty-five

THE NIGHT BURGER PARKING LOT is empty. Not a single car. I park in front of the giant moon and exit my LaPree. Sunlight shines on the faded green brick building. The colorful wall paintings that once displayed cosmic environments with stars and various burger planets now look like one big chalky blotch. I walk along the cracked sidewalk. Hanging on the revolving entrance door is a sign: CLOSED. I hold my hands to my face and peer inside. All the lights are turned off. I press my ear against the glass. No random sound effects. I step back and run to one of the round flying-saucer-top windows. Nothing but black. I return to the entrance door and knock.

"Hello?" I push the door. "Hello!" I shake the door. "HELLO?!"

I head around back to the drive-thru. The outside menu is unreadable. "Hello!" I say into the moon speaker box. "Is anyone there?" No one responds. *"Hello!"*

I follow the white drive-thru lines to the eye of the universe. It's covered with some purple film and sealed shut. I walk back to my LaPree and sit in the driver's seat, staring at the giant moon until the sun eventually disappears and everything around me turns black.

"Light," I say. "Light."

Any second now, the giant moon will come to life and illuminate the night sky.

I wait and wait. Nothing happens.

"Light!" I scream. "FUCKING LIGHT!"

I grab my steering wheel and shake back and forth. Tears roll down my face. I scream. Again and again. Night Burger can't be gone. It's all I have left. Time passes. The moon doesn't light. I'm left in the dark.

I wake to the sun shining on my face. It's hot. I roll down my window. I'm still parked in the Night Burger lot. The building looks the same as it did yesterday: faded, empty, CLOSED. I don't remember falling asleep. I don't remember how I even got to Night Burger. The last thing I recall is escaping Rudy's (I mean, Henry's). Everything after that has felt like a dream. I start my LaPree, reverse, and exit Night Burger. As I drive down Davis Street, I stare at the giant moon in my rearview mirror and watch it get smalller and smaller until it eventually disappears.

I continue on Davis Street to Homestretch Drive and take that to Circle Trail. My mind is no longer in control of my body. I turn onto Dixie Court. "Why are you taking me back here?" I ask myself.

No response.

As I drive past familiar trees and houses, I feel as if I had never left Glenshire and everything over the past six years of my life never actually happened.

I pull into my old driveway and shift into park. The yard looks like a small jungle, and the house looks like something out of a horror movie. The windows are boarded up, the paint's peeling off, and posted on the front door is a sign: DO NOT ENTER. My mind is flooded with old memories of my dad mowing the yard, my mom talking on the phone, and myself riding my gold ten-speed.

My hand opens the car door. "What are you doing?" My legs step out. "Come on!" I walk across the tall grass toward the house. "Didn't you read the sign?" I ask myself. "DO NOT ENTER!"

I carefully climb the steps of the rotting porch and sit at the top. I used to play on the porch when I was little. My mom didn't like me wandering out in the yard by myself, so to keep me on the porch, she told me the grass turned to lava when she wasn't around, and if I walked on it without her there, I would melt. I assumed she was telling the truth but found out she wasn't when this tennis ball I was bouncing got away from me and made its way onto the grass. I stood on the bottom step for a few minutes, contemplating whether the yellow ball was worth melting over. I eventually decided that it was and cautiously stepped onto the green grass. Nothing happened.

I understand why my mom lied to me. It's much easier to tell a kid that they'll melt to death in hot lava than explain why they shouldn't be wandering around the yard unsupervised. Lying is an essential part of adulthood—lying to friends, family, strangers, yourself. I don't think adults can survive in society telling nothing but the truth. The truth kills adults. They'll never admit it, but it's true. The older we get, the more insecure we become, the more angry, the more boring, the more stubborn, the more cautious, the more adult. Unfortunately for us all, there's no escaping this transformation into adulthood. It's a long, sad, and disgusting process that we all have to go through.

A black Ventrex 4x4 pulls into the driveway. *The cops.* I stand. The driver's side door opens, and a tall black-haired woman steps out. Raven.

"Hello, Tom," she says as she closes her car door.

My stomach drops.

"What are you doing here?!" I shout.

She holds her hands high in the air and walks toward me. "I just want to talk."

"You're here to kill me," I say. "Aren't you?"

"I'm not going to kill you, Tom."

I walk backward until my body slams against the front door. I ignore the DO NOT ENTER sign and twist the doorknob. It's locked. Raven stands at the bottom of the rotting porch. My heart's beating like crazy. She takes a step up. Then another. And another.

"Get back!" I yell. "Get back!"

"Please, I just want to talk."

"We have nothing to talk about!"

"My real name isn't Raven," she says. "It's Ruth."

Raven a.k.a. Ruth tells me the same story my mom had told me (back when we were watching soaps) about how they were best friends growing up.

"We were inseparable," she says. "Best friends forever."

"And what happened, again?" I ask.

"Well, your mother met your father, and I got a job."

"Oh, yeah. Something to do with travel, right?"

"That's what I thought," she says. "The company promised me that I'd be traveling far, far away but just stuck me behind a desk far, far away."

"I don't understand. My mom told me that you traveled everywhere."

Raven shakes her head. "I lied. I felt so stupid for taking this supposed travel job that I couldn't bring myself to tell her the truth. The last thing I wanted was your mom thinking that I broke our friendship pact for a lousy desk job."

We sit on the front porch in silence.

"So how'd you end up at Rudy's?" I ask.

"About eight years ago, I finally got the courage to quit that awful job and moved to Cary to be closer to your mom. I thought living nearby would give me the courage to come clean about everything, but I could never bring myself to do it. At that point, the lies were so out of hand, I was convinced that if your mom ever did learn the truth, she would never forgive me and our friendship would be lost forever. I applied to Rudy's because it was one of the only jobs that offered an afternoon shift. My favorite part of the day was watching soaps via telephone with your mom and I needed a job with hours that allowed me to keep that connection."

Raven starts to tear up. "And then when I found out your parents were killed in that terrible Ferris wheel accident, my whole world fell apart. I lived only an hour away and never once stopped by to say hello."

Silence.

"Why are you telling me all this?" I ask.

"I couldn't keep the lie inside me any longer," she says. "I've always wanted to tell you, but I felt so ashamed."

I think of something to say. "My mom really loved those phone conversations."

Raven wipes away her tears and smiles. "Thanks."

Before she leaves, I ask Raven some questions.

Question 1: "So is your real name Raven or Ruth?"

Answer: "Ruth. When I moved to Cary, I realized that I was unhappy being Ruth and started going by Raven."

Question 2: "Why Raven?"

Answer: "Because I am fierce, strong, and intelligent, and if you cross me, I will pluck your eyes out."

Question 3: "So you knew who I was all along?"

Answer: "Sort of. I had an idea, but after initial questioning, I knew it was you."

Question 4: "Is the war over?"

Answer: "No. I doubt it will ever be over."

Question 5: "Am I in any danger?"

Answer: "Somewhat. Make sure to stay at least fifteen miles away from Rudy's for at least three years. You should also consider dyeing your hair and possibly growing a mustache."

☰ ☰ ☰

We walk down the rotting porch and across the tall grass toward Raven's Ventrex 4x4.
"Good luck with everything," I say.
"Thanks. You too."
She opens her car door and gets in.
"You know," she says, "you should talk to Henry."
"But he hates me."
"He doesn't hate you, Tom. He needs you."

She hands me a piece of paper with her telephone number on it and tells me to keep in touch.

"Sure," I say.

She closes her car door, starts the engine, and flies off.

Henry's mom's house is changing back to normal. The zebra yard has been removed and replaced with grass, and the furry steps leading to the front door are once again concrete. I park behind Henry's Calypso Thunder and exit my LaPree.

HONK! HONK!

Henry's mom pulls up in her purple Tulip Convertible.

"Tom!" She exits her car and runs up to me. "Oh, Tom!" she cries. "I don't want him to die!"

"Who?" I ask. "What's going on?"

She grabs my arms and stares into my eyes. "We have to go."

The wind whips my hair and blows in my face. Whenever I ask Henry's mom where we're going, she bursts into tears.

"Where are we going?"

"WAH!" Bursting tears. "WAH!"

We cruise through downtown Glenshire and head east toward Token Village. I haven't been out this way since Cassie and I broke up.

"Where are we going?" I ask again.

"WAH!" More bursting tears. "WAH!"

Her face is wet and smeared with makeup running down her cheeks. I notice that she's not wearing any fur.

"Please, Mrs. Zanta," I say. "Where are we going?"

She semi-manages to pull herself together. "To . . . the Savings . . . and Hospital."

"Why are we going there?" I ask.

"To see Henry!"

The Savings and Hospital is a state-of-the-art combination bank and hospital located in Token Village. I've never been inside, but I've heard great things.

"Is Henry banking or is he hurt?" I ask.

"He's hurt, Tom!" she screams.

As we blow past the Welcome to Token Village sign, Henry's mom explains how she came home from her Fur Addiction meeting yesterday afternoon and found Henry lying unconscious on the living room floor.

"I took him straight to the hospital. I was there all day and night. The doctors sent me home early this morning to rest, but I can't. I can't sleep. I can't eat. I can't . . ." She continues talking but her voice, the wind, and every other sound around me shuts off. I enter my brain. A large screen appears and plays back images from *my* life: Bus stop.

Henry. E-Z-Rests. Music conducting. Bikes. Night Burger. Football friends. High school. Poisoning customers. *Four Seasons.* Car explosion. Fake parents. Community College. Cassie. Teltrox. Sex. Lies. Wallpaper. Apartment. Hellos. TV. Rudy's. The Old Men. The Women's Circle. The Voyeurs. The High School and College Kids. Lisa. Pete. Magic O's. Henry's. Henry's. Henry's. The screen bursts into flames and Henry appears. His mouth moves, but I can't hear him.

"Speak up!" I yell.

He begins to flash. I try to walk over to him but can't move. I have no legs. No body. No arms. Just a head floating in a big empty space.

"SPEAK UP!" I yell again.

Henry flashes more and more until he disappears.

"Tom. Tom. Tom." Henry's mom shakes me awake. "We're here."

We exit the convertible and walk quickly through the bank/hospital entrance doors. A tall, well-dressed, man greets us. "Welcome to the Savings and Hospital," he says. "Would you like to open a checking account today?"

"No!" Henry's mom shouts. "We're not here for banking!"

"My apologies."

We take an elevator to the eighteenth floor. An automated message plays over the speakers. *"Welcome to the Savings and Hospital. Today is free check day. Ask your doctor or bank representative for more information."* Henry's mom stands facing the big steel doors. She holds her rabbit's foot in her hand. *DING!* The doors open. We rush out and walk down one long hallway after another. There are men and women in suits and white doctor coats everywhere. Henry's mom disappears into one of the rooms. My body floats inside, where Henry's lying on a hospital bed. His body is hooked up to all these machines. *Beep. Beep. Beep.* His eyes are closed and he has tubes coming out of his mouth and nose.

"Hey," I say to Henry. He doesn't respond.

I look around the room. It's decorated with various posters advertising low interest rates, cash back rewards, zero percent APR. A woman with curly hair sits at a desk a few feet away. Behind her is a clear plastic tube that stretches from the floor to the ceiling.

"Have a great day, Mr. Benzy," she says into her headset as she places one of those clear banking capsules in the long, clear tube. *Whoosh!* The capsule disappears.

I focus back on Henry. He looks like he's asleep on his E-Z-Rest.

"Henry," I say.

Someone places their hand on my shoulder. "He needs to rest, Tom," says Henry's teary-eyed mom.

"Henry," I say again.

"He can't *hear* you," says the bearded doctor.

"HENRY!" I yell.

The doctor grabs my arm. "Please," he says. "Yelling won't wake him."

I push the doctor away and shake Henry's lifeless body.

"WAKE UP! WAKE UP! WAKE UP!"

WAH! WAH! WAH!

An alarm sounds. A bunch of security guards rush in and tackle me to the floor.

"HENRY!!!" I scream.

The curly-haired woman at the desk continues working.

"Have a great day, Mr. Kron."

She places another banking capsule in the clear plastic tube. *Whoosh!* The capsule disappears.

twenty-six

"**I** HAVE to quit."

Henry's eyes remained glued to the TV and his body to the E-Z-Rest.

"Are you even listening to me?" I asked.

"Yeah."

I sat up on the blue couch. "So what do you think about that?"

"You've only been working there a few months."

"I know," I said. "But if I stay any longer, I think I'll go crazy."

"It can't be that bad," Henry replied.

"You heard the stories. It's horrible. The other day—"

"Quiet."

Henry stared at the television. He was watching this movie called *Stand Up* about a guy in a wheelchair who makes this birthday wish that he could stand up. Next thing you know, the guy's standing up and walking around. The whole town makes a big deal over his supposed triumph, and he ends up becoming this hotshot celebrity. First off, the movie is called *Stand Up* not *Stand Up and Walk Around*. If this guy only wished to stand up, he should *only* be able to stand up. Second, birthday wishes aren't real. The guy was probably faking his paralysis the entire time. If I made a sequel to this movie, I would call it *Sit Down*, and it would be about how much of an asshole the guy is for tricking people into thinking he couldn't walk.

"This movie is horrible," I said.

"It's not horrible," Henry replied.

"It looks horrible."

"You don't even know what horrible looks like."

"Well, you don't know what horrible sounds like."

"What's that mean?" Henry asked.

"It means that if I tell you Rudy's is horrible and you disagree with me, then you don't know what horrible *sounds* like, and if I think a movie you're watching is horrible and you disagree, then according to you, I don't know what horrible *looks* like."

"Then I guess we know nothing about each other."

"Exactly."

The apartment intercom buzzed.

"Who's that?" I asked.

No response.

The intercom buzzed again.

"Answer it!" screamed Henry.

"Why can't you?"

He pointed at the television. "I'm in the middle of something *horrible.*"

🍔 🍔 🍔

I got up off the blue couch and pushed the Talk button on the intercom. "Hello."

"Good afternoon," a firm voice replied, "I'm looking for Tom Mitchell."

"Who is it?" I asked.

"Officer Kendal with the Glenshire Police Department."

Night Burger. Bad thoughts. Poisoning customers. I released the Talk button and looked at Henry. "What are the cops doing here?"

"Hopefully, taking you away." he replied.

I took a deep breath and once again pushed the Talk button. "How can I help you?"

"May I come up?" asked the officer.

My heart began beating faster and faster. I could see it jumping up and down through my shirt.

"Hello? Anyone there?"

"Yes," I replied.

"May I come up, please?"

"Sure."

I pushed the Door button on the intercom and ran into the bathroom. I grabbed some bandages from the cabinet and stuck them to my face. If Henry's dumb movie had taught me anything of value, it was that normal-functioning people are oftentimes kinder to people with injuries.

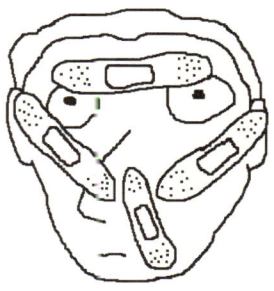

KNOCK! KNOCK! KNOCK!

I secured my face bandages and opened the door.

"Tom Mitchell?" said this gloomy-looking officer.

My brain screamed *run*, but my legs wouldn't listen. "Yes."

"May I come inside?"

"Okay."

The officer entered the apartment and shut the door.

"This is my roommate, Henry." I don't typically do introductions, but I wanted to shift focus to the long-haired, bearded freak sitting on the gray recliner.

"Hello, Henry," said the officer.

Henry aimed the remote and turned up the volume.

"Is there somewhere we can talk in private?"

I knew what cops did when they got suspected criminals alone in a room. "This is the best place," I said. "It's a small apartment."

"Have you been in some kind of accident recently?" the officer asked, eyeing the bandages on my face.

"Yeah," I replied. "Um . . . bird attack."

"Sorry to hear that."

I looked down at the carpet. "The doctor says my face may never be the same."

"My mother was attacked by a bird once. Lost her left eye." Awkward pause. "Anyway . . ." The cop removed his hat and explained how my fake parents had been involved in a Ferris wheel accident. Supposedly the big center bolt somehow loosened, causing the giant wheel to unhinge from its A-frame mount and roll off down the street. The police and fire department tried their best to safely contain the giant wheel, but due to its enormous size and high speed of travel, they were unsuccessful in their attempts. Eventually the wheel made its way to Long Way Down Cliff and rolled off the edge. All twenty-eight poor souls aboard the family-friendly carnival ride perished.

I stood there a moment, unsure how to react.

"I'm sorry," said the officer. "I know how difficult this must be for you."

He apologized again and again and told me how important it was that I stay strong. A part of me didn't believe his story. He was lying. I thought about crying, but no tears came out. I felt sad, but not the kind of sadness I should have been feeling. It was like two strangers had died. I never knew much about my fake parents. I knew their names, where they worked, what they ate, and other stuff like that, but I rarely talked to them about their lives or thoughts or anything meaningful. They didn't know much about my life, either.

"Are you going to be okay?" asked the officer.

I nodded.

He explained what would happen over the next few days and gave me the name of the doctor who helped his mother. "Venkin. Edward V. Venkin. The guy specializes in bird attacks. You should see my mother's left eye. Can't even tell it's a fake."

"Thanks."

The officer opened the apartment door. "You take care of him, Henry, okay?"

Henry aimed the remote and turned down the volume.

"Stay strong, Tom," he said as he exited the apartment. "Stay strong."

I closed the door behind him and sat back down on the blue couch.

"I'm sorry, Tom," Henry said.

I ripped one of the bandages off my face. "Who the hell dies on a Ferris wheel?"

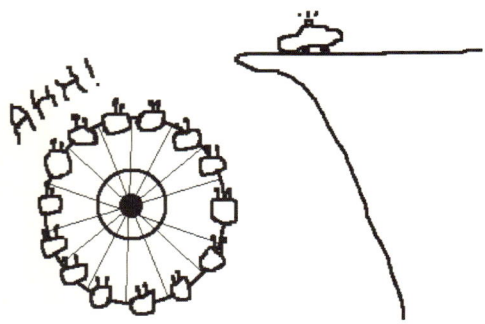

The bank took the house, the cars, the clothes, and everything else my fake parents owned. Supposedly they had purchased an island property awhile back and still owed money on it. I tried to get some stuff out of my bedroom but was denied access.

"Sorry, Mr. Mitchell," said the robotic bank representative over the phone, "but everything now belongs to the Always Trust Bank."

The funeral was small and cheap. One shared wooden casket. One miniature tombstone. They were buried at Last Stop Cemetery in Glenshire. No one showed up. I hung around and watched the big crane lower the shabby casket into the ground. I heard a story once about a man who buried his dead wife in his flower garden because he thought he could grow her back to life. It didn't work. The man got himself in some trouble with the law over it. I don't think he got any jail time, but I'm pretty sure he ruined his reputation with the neighbors.

All of the employees at Rudy's heard about the Ferris wheel accident. They talked about it constantly: how it happened, who was responsible, and mainly, what the victims where thinking as they plummeted hundreds of feet to their deaths. Since my fake parents and I had different last names, no one had any idea that I was somewhat related to the victims in car number three: Edmond and Victoria Lexington. I was happy the employees didn't know, as I didn't want them knowing anything about me. The only person who knew about my fake parents' death was Henry. He took it pretty seriously, and to pay his respects, kept the TV volume turned down a few notches.

"If you need me to turn it down any lower, just say the word," he said. "I understand what you're going through."

The death of my fake parents actually brought Henry and I closer together. We stopped arguing as much and got back to talking and watching TV like we used to. I think Henry liked that my fake parents were dead. We now had something in common: his dad and my fake parents were all killed in horrible accidents. I still thought about my lack of sadness over the tragedy and wondered if I'd be sadder if the people who died had been my *real* parents instead of my *fake* parents. I asked Henry about it, and he broke it down for me.

"Basically, a fake parent is like a pet gerbil," he said. "Sure, you feel kind of sad when it dies, but at the same time, it was just a gerbil. However, in your case, you lost two fake parents, so that's like losing two gerbils, or a really cool dog."

Before I knew it, a whole month had passed. Everything was squared away. My fake parents were buried, the bank stuff was worked out, and I was now the proud owner of an island property.

"When are you going to visit?" Henry asked.

"I'm not sure." I stretched out onto the blue couch. "I have to work at Rudy's a whole year before I get any vacation."

Henry sat on his E-Z-Rest, flipping through channels. "It will give you time to save."

"I wish my fake parents were rich like your dad."

"Money doesn't solve all your problems."

"At least you don't have to work at a stupid grocery store where the employees do nothing but fight all the time, and the customers do nothing but complain."

"I think you make it sound worse than it actually is."

"If you don't think it's so bad, then apply."

"I can't."

"Why not?"

"Look at me."

I looked at him. "Just shave and cut your hair."

"It's a lot harder than that."

That was always his excuse.

"Well, until you work at Rudy's, I don't want you telling me how working there isn't that bad. You have no idea what it's like. I hate it! You hear me?! IT'S FUCKING HORRIBLE!"

Henry stopped talking and stared at the TV. I didn't understand why I was getting so angry at him. Henry was the *only* person on this planet who I had left. If anything happened to him, or if he didn't want to be my friend anymore, I don't know what I would do.

"Sorry for yelling," I said. "If you want, you can turn the TV volume back up to normal."

"You sure?" Henry asked.

"Yeah . . . I think my fake parents would have wanted it that way."

twenty-seven

"**I** TOOK A BULLET for you, Jess!"

"That was your decision, Antonio!"

"You'd be dead if it weren't for me!"

"You may have saved my life, but you will never save my heart!"

RING! RING! RING!

I run into the kitchen and grab the cordless. "Hello?"

"Hey, Tom." It's Henry. "What are you doing?"

"I was just watching *Four Seasons*." I turn off the TV and sit back down on the blue couch.

"Do you want me to let you go?" he asks.

"No, I'm not really buying this Jess and Antonio love story."

"Sorry to hear that."

"It's okay," I tell him. "Ricardo and Emilia are steamy enough."

"Did you eat lunch already?" he asks.

"No, why?"

He tells me there's this new restaurant that opened up where Night Burger used to be and asks if I'd be interested in checking it out.

"Sure."

"Cool," he says. "I'll pick you up at one."

After Henry got released from the Savings and Hospital, he was sent directly over to the New Man or Woman Rehabilitation Center. I didn't see or talk to him during his entire stay, as the center did not allow any phone calls or visitors. He's been back home living with his mom for about a week. We spoke on the phone a few times, but today will be the first time in, like, three months that we're actually going to see one another. The last time I saw Henry was at the Savings and Hospital. He was unconscious and hooked up to all those machines. I wonder if he looks the same. He probably won't recognize me. I've been bleaching my hair blond and have a pretty thick mustache. I don't necessarily like the look, but considering what happened at Rudy's, I have no choice. My life is still in danger. I try not to go out in public much. It's a good thing I stole all that toilet paper.

I still live in the same apartment. It's going all right. For a while, the place was haunted. I'd be asleep in my bedroom and wake up to these reclining noises coming from the living room. Eventually I came to the conclusion that the E-Z-Rest was possessed, so I dragged it out into the hallway one night and left it in front of someone else's apartment door. Hopefully, the person thought it was a gift, as the act clearly went against my No-Bother Policy. Whatever the case, the recliner's not there anymore.

My favorite television show is still *Four Seasons* (I purchased a set of bunny ears from Eel Ed's Electronics). Watching it reminds me of my mom and brings me back to that summer after I graduated high school. I find myself thinking about my dead parents more and more lately. Every so often, I'll visit their tiny tomb-stone to say hello and leave a fresh pair of pantyhose.

The following letter is dated November 3, 2001, and sits on the kitchen counter:

Dear real mom,

This is your son, Tom Mitchell. I am doing okay. The people who raised me have died in a horrible Ferris wheel accident. Through their death, I inherited an island property. I have yet to visit but hear it's beautiful. For the past six years I have been working at Rudy's Grocery, where I stocked food, gathered carts, and dealt with annoying customers. Recently, I was fired for refusing to join one of the three main employee groups who were at war with one another and also, more likely, for stealing toilet paper. Don't worry. I am not in jail. I currently live in an apartment in Dire. I had a roommate, but he got sick. His mom sends checks each month to cover his portion of the rent. I have been watching a lot of TV and contemplating my next move. Eventually, my savings will run out, and I will have to return to work. I am thinking about one of those work-from-home jobs. Do you have any experience in that field? I actually saw a new Mr. Jim infomercial the other night. He's now selling a Get Rich Quick video. It sounded promising, but I didn't pick up the phone and call this time. Anyway, that's about it. Hope you are doing okay.

Sincerely,

Tom

P.S. After rereading this letter, I realized that you might not know who Mr. Jim is, but just know that he wears a bad toupee and his products do NOT work.

Before leaving, I call Raven to tell her the good news.
"Henry and I are going out for lunch."
"That's great!" she says. "Call me after to chat!"
"You got it!"
I talk to Raven every day. We've become great friends. She's currently hiding out on the island property that I inherited from my parents. According to her, the Old Men won the war. Supposedly, they created some highly poisonous prescription medication mixture and used it to contaminate the break room water fountain.

"All the women started getting sick," Raven explained. "No one could figure out why."

"What about the Voyeurs?" I asked. "Were they getting sick?"

"Not a single one."

Eventually, Raven captured an old man and tortured the truth out of him, but by that time, it was too late. The Women's Circle was down to only eight members. Raven, realizing the group's inevitable defeat, set up a secret meeting with Walter and Gary and announced the group's surrender.

"The women were outraged," she told me. "They blamed me for the loss."

Raven was chased out of Rudy's and placed on the Women Circle's Top Five Most Wanted List. She abandoned her apartment in Cary and escaped to the island property, where she lives in a small bungalow and goes by the name Erica Flowers.

One of the women, still in communication with Raven, updates her on what's going on. Supposedly, the Old Men are now the largest group and have employees stationed on the grocery floor, cash registers, and of course, in the back room. Customers have been complaining about the slow service but are very happy with the good old-fashioned small talk.

The Voyeurs, who Raven believes were in cahoots with the Old Men, now have free range to spy on customers anythroughout the store. They even have access to the back room.

As far as The Women's Circle goes, they are in rebuild mode. A tough and hardheaded new hire named Granite has stepped up as their leader and promises complete Rudy's control in less than a year.

"What's going on with Pete?" I asked.

"According to my inside source, he got both his ears pierced and has been hanging with the High School and College Kids."

Henry picks me up in his Calypso Thunder. He has a short beard and medium-length hair. He doesn't look nearly as adult as he used to.

"Nice mustache," he tells me as I enter his car.

"Thanks."

As we drive up Davis Street, I see two kids riding their bikes along the side of the road. If they're going to the new restaurant, they're a little late. The best restaurant that ever existed in Glenshire is gone forever. Night Burger came at a time we needed it and took off when we had no use for it anymore. It was like an alien ship that flew down from outer space, hung out for a bit, and left, never to return. The aliens were probably just seeing what the fast food business was like before they started one up in space. They probably took off because of the customers. I wouldn't be surprised.

"There it is!" says Henry.

I look out the windshield and see a white sign with some cursive writing. "What's that say?" I ask.

"I'm not sure," Henry replies.

We drive closer.

"Italian Accents."

The building looks like a small house. It's made of brown brick and has a normal, triangle-style rooftop. The windows are square and the front door is a standard push/pull.

"Do you think they have a drive-thru?" I ask.

"I doubt it," Henry says as he kills the engine.

We exit the car and walk along the pristine sidewalk. Before entering the restaurant, I look out toward Davis Street and watch as the two kids on bikes stop in front of the main sign, shake their heads, and ride off.

"You coming?" Henry holds open the entrance door.

"Yeah."

The inside is dimly lit and classical music plays over the speakers. The walls are painted red and decorated with framed pictures of bread, spaghetti, and pizza. Tables with center candles are scattered throughout the dining area and a classy bar lined with various liquor bottles is pushed off in the corner. Directly in front of us stands a wooden podium with a sign that reads: Please Wait To Be Seated.

Some guy wearing black pants and a white long-sleeved dress shirt appears. "Velcome to Italían Accénts," he says. "I am Marío." He smiles and grabs two menus from behind the podium. "This way."

We follow him through the restaurant, passing a young couple, four middle-aged women, and three fat guys. They're all very quiet.

"Voilà," announces Mario. "The perféct table."

Henry and I sit down. Mario hands us our menus.

"Thanks," Henry and I both say.

"Drinks?"

"Water's fine," says Henry.

"I'll have the same."

Mario places his hands together, nods, and leaves. I set my menu on the wooden table and stare at the red walls until I can see the cosmic wall paintings and round flying-saucer-top windows and fueling station and starlit ceiling and Kalmax and the Burger Prince and—

"What are you thinking about ordering?" Henry asks.

"Not sure."

I pick up my menu and flip through the laminated pages. They have everything: pasta, pizza, sandwiches, soups, salads. All the food names are normal. Spaghetti, chicken parmesan, minestrone. I flip to the back of the menu and browse the drink selection: pop, diet pop, tea, coffee, beer, wine. It's all very ordinary.

Mario returns with two waters and a basket of bread. "Veady to ordér?"

I look at Henry. He nods.

"We're ready."

Henry orders the lasagna and I order a small cheese pizza.

"Anyving else?"

"That will be all."

"Perfécto!" Mario collects our menus and walks off.

"Do you think this place is really Italian?" I ask Henry as I grab a piece of bread.

He looks around. "It looks Italian."

"I guarantee it's not," I say. "You can buy this stuff any-where—the pictures and music and candles. It seems fake. I don't think our waiter's accent is real, either."

Henry grabs a piece of bread. "Does it matter if it's real?"

"Are you talking about the restaurant or the accent?"

"Both."

I think about it for a second. "I guess not. As long as the food's good, I guess." I take a bite of the bread. "I like the bread."

≅ ≅ ≅

"Lasagna for you, sir . . . pízza for you, sir. Anyving else?"

"Some more bread, please," I say.

Mario frowns and walks off. He's probably upset about the additional bread request. I think the rule is one basket per table. I'm going to have to give him an extra dollar tip or something.

"How's your pizza?" Henry asks.

"Good," I say. "How about your lasagna?"

"Best meal I've had in awhile."

He tells me how the food at the New Man or Woman Rehabilitation Center was terrible and how the dinners really beat up his stomach.

"You probably had an angry chef," I said.

"What?"

"Typically, if the person cooking your food is angry, they will put their feelings of rage and frustration into the meal by adding too much seasoning, cooking the food for too long, and so on."

"Interesting," says Henry. "This one time I ordered the meat loaf, and after I ate it, I felt like I just played an intense game of football."

"Yep," I say. "Definitely an angry chef."

Mario sets a fresh basket of bread on the table. "How is everyving?" he asks.

"Good."

"Perfécto!" he leaves.

Henry tells me that he's thinking about going to college.

"Really," I say. "What do you want to study?"

"I'm not sure." He takes a bite of his lasagna. "Any suggestions?"

"Um . . . business."

"Maybe."

I eat another slice of pizza.

"What about you?" Henry asks. "What's your plan?"

"I'm not sure," I say. "I'm going to have to get a new job eventually."

Henry lowers his head. "I'm sorry about everything that went on at Rudy's."

"It's okay . . . I'm sorry, too."

We sit in silence. I want to ask him about *the incident* but I'm not sure if it's appropriate. I should be able to ask Henry anything. After all, we are best friends. I look around the restaurant. The four middle-aged women and young couple have left, Mario's in back, and the three fat guys are sleeping face-first in their pasta.

"How did you end up in the hospital?" I ask.

Henry's face turns red.

"Sorry," I say. "You don't have to tell me."

He takes a deep breath. "I swallowed a bunch of pills."

"What kind of pills?"

"They were these things my mom had," he says.

"What happened when you took them?"

"Nothing at first, but about ten minutes in, I started getting really nervous about furry things."

"What do you mean?"

"You know that coyote blanket my mom bought me?"

"Yeah."

"Well, I was lying in my bed wrapped up in it, and it started to scare me." Henry continues. "I threw it off and ran out of my bedroom. Then I started hearing the *noises*."

"What noises?"

"Animal noises," he says. "Angry animal noises. Lions, tigers, zebras, all types—crying and howling. I tried covering my ears, but the noises just got louder and louder. Next thing I know, I'm on the ground shaking and I can't move and I can't breathe and it feels like someone's ripping off my skin. I wanted to scream, it hurt so bad, but I couldn't. Eventually, I must have passed out, because the next thing I know, I wake up in the hospital. I guess I slipped into a coma."

"What kind of pills is your mom taking?" I ask.

"I found out they were anti-fur pills," Henry says. "For my mom's fur addiction."

"I didn't know they made stuff like that."

"Me either," Henry says. "I've been talking to a therapist about everything. It's helped a lot. I'm feeling much better."

"Why'd you do it?" I ask.

Henry stares at the plain ceiling. He looks like he's about to cry. "I don't know," he says. "It was a lot of things. My dad, my life, everything. I wasn't happy."

Pause.

"Have you ever thought about it?" he asks.

"Thought about what?"

"You know," he says. "Killing yourself."

"Yeah, I guess, sometimes."

"How come you never did it?"

"I just always thought that things would get better somehow," I say. "I also don't know how I'd even do it. I couldn't stab myself, because that would hurt too much. Jumping off a building would leave a big mess for somebody to clean up. I'd also want to die in a cool way."

"I hate myself for attempting it."

Another pause.

"I hate myself, too, for a lot of things. I don't have attempting suicide on the list, but I'm definitely not happy about everything."

One final pause.

"I hate my name," I tell him.

"You never told me you hate your name."

"I don't think it has a good ring to it," I say. "Anyway, everyone has stuff they hate about themselves. You're not the only one."

"Thanks, Tom."

We finish our meals in silence and listen to the classical music play over the restaurant speakers. It's weird how such insane people can make such beautiful music.

As we wait for the check, Henry tosses out the idea of moving back into the apartment.

"I can't stand living with my mom," he says. "Ever since she stopped wearing fur, she's been acting weird."

I tell him about this show I saw about people who wear fur and how it changes them as people. "According to the show, wearing animal fur gives you the traits of that animal."

We list off all the different furs that we've seen his mom wear.

"Rabbit."

"Squirrel."

"Cheetah."

"Polar bear."

"Lion."

"Kangaroo."

"So according to this show, my mom's turning into all of these animals?" asks Henry.

"Yep."

Mario clears our plates and places a small black folder on the table. "Whenever you're veady."

We split the bill and leave a few bucks for tip. I toss in an extra dollar for the second basket of bread.

"Can I ask you something?" I ask Henry as we stand to leave.

"Sure."

"You won't get mad, right?"

"No."

"Were you ever together with Lisa?"

"What do you mean?" he asks. "Like, dating?"

"Yeah."

"No way," he says. "I'm into blondes, and besides, Lisa has a serious boyfriend."

"Really?"

"You didn't know that?"

"No."

"She talked about him constantly. It was actually kind of annoying."

"Yeah," I say. "I can't stand when people talk about their boyfriend or girlfriend all the time. I don't think those couples are really happy."

"It's like they're hiding something."

"Exactly."

We push in our chairs and walk through the dining room.

"Thank you for dining at Italían Accénts," Mario says as we exit. "Have a vonderful day."

I still think his accent's fake.

≋ ≋ ≋

Outside, some guy with long white hair and sunglasses leans against Henry's Calypso Thunder.

"Is that . . . Roy?"

"Who?" Henry asks.

"The guy who owned Night Burger," I say. "They used to have a picture of him hanging up in the office."

He spots us and walks over.

"Tom Mitchell and Henry Zanta," he says. "Pleasure to meet you both."

"How do you know our names?" Henry asks.

"I know a lot more than that." Roy smiles. "I'm glad things finally worked out between you two. Your friendship is very important. I didn't know how much longer we were going to have to stick around."

"Why'd you close down Night Burger?" I ask.

Roy laughs. "It was time to move on." He turns and walks away. "Enjoy Italian Accénts!"

Henry and I look at each other and then back at Roy.

"Where'd he go?" Henry asks.

"He was *just* here," I say.

We search the entire parking lot. Nothing. He completely vanished. I even went back inside the restaurant to see if he was hiding out in the dining room. Nope.

"You saw him, right?" I ask Henry as we step into his Calypso Thunder.

"Yeah," Henry replies.

"He just disappeared!"

"I know!"

Henry starts the car. I buckle my seat belt and stare out the window. I couldn't believe what just happened. It was the first time either one of us had ever seen a real-life alien.

- Acknowledgments -

I don't think Tom would want to thank anyone; however, I would like to give a quick thanks to the following people:

Nancy Beckett, for teaching me how to become a writer as well as a reader. Your guidance and continued support has meant the world to me. Without you and your Lakeside Writing Studio, this book would not exist.

Lakeside writers Catherine Postilion, David Finch, the late Mary Scruggs, Adina Kabaker, Kelly Kennoy, Ann Lamas, Sylvie Sadarnac, Cathy Scherer, Sheila Flaherty, and Laurie Cunningham, for all of your encouragement and valuable feedback.

Paul Malyszek, for being the first person to read my novel from start to finish. Martin J. Murphy, for helping me design my website and book cover. Nathan Contreras, for drawing my bio picture. Lydia Rivera, for supporting me during the writing process. Hunter S. Thompson, who I never met, but showed me that writing has a place for the weird.

My wonderful editor, Rachel Lee Cherry.

My mom and dad.

My friends and family.

Bradley Dilger, for teaching me how to write clearly and professionally. Jeff Kleinman and Jackie Carlson, for your expert feedback and words of encouragement. Luke Cella, for being a cool boss.

Lastly, thanks to everyone who donated to my publishing fundraiser: Linus Lee, John Wefler, Dénes Juhász, Iris Chu, Sarah Kabli, Al Candelario, Lydia Rivera, Brian Lode Jr., Veronica Diaz, Stephanie Lode, Brian Lode Sr., Jordan Rolih, Catherine Postilion, Tom Donnelly, Dan Rivera, Kristen Rolih, Fallon Iverson, Sheila Flaherty, Melissa Odom, Ann Lamas, Erin Decaire, Mark Hendrickx, David Finch, Dianne Rolih, Rebecca Cannon, Christina Igaraividez, Kevin Stanton, Danielle Sarna, John Katsibubas, Martin J. Murphy, Tony and Liz Chavez, Shannon Plecki, Nicholas Simpson, Ramon Alvarado, and Dr. Kristen Wells.

That's enough of that.

JASON SARNA grew up in the suburbs of Illinois. He has not won any writing awards or prizes. This is his first novel.

babushkaheaven.com

11820618R00192

Made in the USA
San Bernardino, CA
31 May 2014